TALABARSKE

TALABARSKE

The True Story of Two Brothers

With One Extraordinary Bond

Finding Life After Ruin

In World War II

GINNY ZAPAR COHEN

WITH LUBOMYR ZAPAR

Mill City Press, Inc.
322 First Avenue N, 5th floor
Minneapolis, MN 55401
612.455.2293
www.millcitypublishing.com

ISBN-13: 978-1-62652-450-7
LCCN: 2013918841

Typeset by James Arneson

Printed in the United States of America

*To my dad, Lubomyr, and all of 'The Others'
we've loved and lost in the trenches of life.*

Contents

PREFACE　　　　　　　　　　　　　　　　　　xi

PROLOGUE:　Winter, 1944　　　　　　　　　　xv

CHAPTER 1:　The Conscription　　　　　　　　1

CHAPTER 2:　The Others　　　　　　　　　　13

CHAPTER 3:　The Return　　　　　　　　　　23

CHAPTER 4:　Love & War　　　　　　　　　　31

CHAPTER 5:　The Burning　　　　　　　　　49

CHAPTER 6:　Out of the Ashes　　　　　　　61

CHAPTER 7:　Caught in the Vise　　　　　　69

CHAPTER 8:　Taking Chances　　　　　　　77

CHAPTER 9:　Angels Among Demons　　　　89

CHAPTER 10:　The War Still Raging　　　　　99

CHAPTER 11:　Shelter In The Storm　　　　107

CHAPTER 12:　The River Crossing　　　　　119

CHAPTER 13:　Family Treasure　　　　　　127

CHAPTER 14:　The Round Up　　　　　　　131

CHAPTER 15:　Friend or Foe?　　　　　　　137

CHAPTER 16:　Only Luckier　　　　　　　　147

CHAPTER 17:　Repatriation　　　　　　　　155

CHAPTER 18:　Children in a Parallel World　165

CHAPTER 19: Development   175

CHAPTER 20: The Naked Angel   183

CHAPTER 21: Bridge Collapse   189

CHAPTER 22: The News   195

CHAPTER 23: The Voyage   199

CHAPTER 24: America   205

EPILOGUE   211

Boldy 'gainst the current
Swim the stream across
Till you die, with courage
Bear the heavy cross...

—Iwan Franko, *Against the Stream*

PREFACE

The grave of Iwan Franko in Lychakivskiy Cemetery, Lviv,
Ukraine, photo credit: Ginny Zapar Cohen

WHAT STARTED OUT AS A FAMILY history has morphed into family legend. For many years I had heard bits and pieces of this legend told by my Babcia...my grandmother, Daria. But the stories were never coherently strung together until my dad, Lyiubchyk, began to patiently transcribe them all into a diary. He called the chronicle of his family's escape from Ukraine *Our Bonus Lives*. He began writing it shortly after returning from his first-and-last trip back to Ukraine, when he was 70 years old.

He and I made this trek together in 2010 and, during our travels in Lviv, stumbled upon the grave of Iwan Franko, one of the most famous poets and writers of Ukraine, in Lychakivskiy cemetery. We were told by our English speaking guide about a legend that said if you rubbed the stone of Franko's grave it would turn you into a writer. So naturally, Dad and I did just that. We looked up at each other and I said, "Now I guess we need to go write something."

Oddly enough, upon our return, Dad started writing his account of his family's escape and I, inspired by the magnitude of it all, began transforming his diary into this novel. So together we began laying out our book, *Talabarske*.

Each chapter of this book begins with italicized words, words taken directly from Dad's *Our Bonus Lives*. My narrative follows. I hope it does justice to Dad's words and reflects the facts of his life—a life filled with turmoil, grace, and sheer luck of survival.

Unfortunately, we were only about eight chapters in when Dad was diagnosed with a terminal form of Lymphoma. In December of 2012, he passed away. What he left behind, though, was a magnificent gift. Not just of family history and memories, but documentation for the world at large of yet another family that surmounted great odds to betray death and live out lives of happiness—not just for themselves but in order to serve humanity and teach people to relish the dawn of each new day. If they could live through all of this, surely life's not too bad and death not too hard to cheat. That is something that never left Dad. His family struggled so hard to overcome the prison of war that he truly never took one day for granted and he fought for every second of his life until the bitter end.

Even facing death, Dad was a lover of life—he died with a tear streaming down his cheek. He wasn't ready to go. He loved this world and all that he had been through to take hold of it, to serve it, to play his part. So here it is. Proof that even in absence, life continues...and inspiration never ceases.

I love you, Dad.

PROLOGUE

Winter, 1944

IT WAS WHITE AS FAR AS the eye could see. The five wives and their children sat in the tattered covered wagons, held hostage by their own fear and silence. They had already waited nearly two hours—the snowdrifts rose to the top of the wagon wheels. The horses were restless, shifting from side to side in anxious anticipation of their continuing journey westward. But nothing moved. The air had that steely smell of snowfall and even through the bitter cold the wives felt nothing but crushing fear. Time stood still.

They could see dim candlelight coming from inside the cabin and a small plume of smoke rising from the chimney. The caravan sat idle in front of the makeshift border patrol about a quarter of a mile away—just far enough for the ladies to be able to remain fixated on the movements inside, yet too far to hear or see anything that was going on within the stone walls.

One hour in, they could take it no more. They decided to trudge through the drifts, children on their hips, and beg the guard to let their husbands go.

Cautiously, Daria opened the door to find her beloved husband, Iwan, and his brother, Petro, lined up against the back wall with three other husbands from their caravan. It was an ominous sight—perhaps the prelude to their execution. Daria couldn't help but remember Iwan's final plea before they had chosen this risky path for their young family: One way or another they would all die or survive together—but they would not give up. They would do everything in their power to claim this life that was theirs.

They belonged to no one.

CHAPTER 1

The Conscription

Iwan Pavlovych Zapar (Left), born November 1, 1910 and
Petro Pavlovych Zapar (Right), born August 22, 1908.
Photo courtesy of the Zapar family.

AS IS COMMON IN *most families, a certain amount of migration
occurs due to life's circumstances—survival, career, random choices
made by individuals, and unknown fates over which we appear to
have limited, if any, control. We seem to be guided by a force we may
not acknowledge or understand, but that nevertheless has a role in our
present and future lives.*

They say that souls travel in packs—swirls of energy longing to clutch on to that which is already known, or unknown. Like magnets, their force spans days, decades, lifetimes, and maybe even generations through family, romance, chance meetings, and sometimes even fate. These were two souls living not for the warmth of the sun's rays, or the feeling you get when you take that first sip of steaming espresso on a cold day, but for each other. They were brothers and they were two souls that lived life backwards. To earn life, they first had to die.

•

These two brothers lived a typical early-twentieth-century Ukrainian life with only the occasional luxury of hot food or warm clothes, but they made do. If it was bitter cold and they didn't have socks, well, they tore some linens in strips to wrap around their feet. Most of their needs were met, but not with any extravagance. Wants—well, they weren't even a figment of the imagination. But these two brothers were grateful for what they had and, most importantly, for the blessing of family.

The younger of the two, Iwan, as his name augured, was the more gracious and serious one—Petro focused on his own amusement when he wasn't tied to chores or other responsibilities. Although only two years separated the brothers, Petro deferred to Iwan's good sense when it came to making important decisions. This is a naturally occurring phenomenon of brotherhood that arises through the process of trial and error, and one that, for these two, was settled early on with Iwan's facility for avoiding spankings. Head down, hands callused, he did as he was told. And Petro simply followed suit.

The brothers could usually be found tending to chickens, cattle, gardens, or schoolwork but were able to steal an occasional idle afternoon wandering the thick grain fields together. As was the Ukrainian custom of the time, their Mama would send them off with safety pins carefully tucked inside their clothing for the purpose of warding off evil spirits. Lounging amongst the grain stalks, they crafted their own language, speaking to each other backwards so quickly and with such skill that, to the casual listener, it sounded like childish gibberish. They quickly became so fluent that no one understood their language—they soon fell in to using it anytime they spoke with each other. Eventually, they came to call this language *Talabarske*.

Their parents lived an unspectacular life—a mostly gray existence. They worked hard and had no time for even simple pleasures. Lenin's Bolsheviks were attempting to mobilize the working class in both the Russian and Ukrainian governments to rebel against the Tsarist autocracy of Russia. The air was heavy with stale indignation and a looming sense of spiraling conflict. Leading through fear—and extermination of all non-supporters by firing squad—they beguiled their followers with empty promises of taking land from the rich and distributing it to the poor—a process they referred to as *collectivization*. In reality, the peasants received nothing while communist sympathizers and corrupt loyalists reaped the rewards of land and money.

After World War I, the Communist Party infiltrated all levels of government, leaving a trail of fear and distrust—even within the families of prominent members. No one felt safe speaking, not even to their own children, for fear that they had been commissioned by government officials to extort information from them and divulge everything they learned. Failure to report subversive chatter or disloyalty was punishable by death. The fortunate *traitors* would be shot, while the *survivors* would be given harsh and miserable punishments in unbearably cold Siberian labor camps with nothing but harsh work and deliberate starvation to fill their time. Siberia's remote location and bitter clime insured that escape would not be feasible.

Disloyal citizens were visited by communist henchmen in the middle of the night and often executed in front of their families or escorted to the nearest party headquarters never to be seen or heard from again. Terror, fear, and force quelled even the most resolute resistance.

The days of Talabarske quickly ended and even though Petro and Iwan had begun studies in nearby Kamyanets-Podilsky, world events precluded the luxury of study.

•

"Well, here we are, Petro," Iwan muttered, staring at the piece of paper carelessly, by all appearances, left on their front door. Iwan could feel the paper fluttering in his trembling fingers, unsure of how to feel. "How can such an important piece of paper be so casually notched to our front door? By duty or damnation those who have sold their souls have come knocking for ours. Petro, do you understand the severity of this? Do you?"

His eyes glazed, Petro's gaze fell in a knowing resignation. "*Tse ploho, braty*. It is bad, brother. I know."

"We can't go. We can't stay. We are dead. Dead to this village and dead to our parents. But we can't go," Iwan stammered.

Like a fire, this notice—although anticipated—scalded the very core of the brothers' souls—their hearts filled with angst. They felt the very breadth of communism—life was out of their control. They had to choose. Would they be counted among the dutiful or the damned? It was May 1, 1931, and Petro and Iwan—23 and 21, respectively—were consigned to report for duty in the Communist Army. They had three days to report. If they didn't they risked death by firing squad.

"We have no choice, Iwan," Petro said. "If we don't go they will kill us."

"Then we must leave." Iwan stood, resolute.

"They'll take our parents, Iwan. Don't you understand? They will kill us and they will kill them. We can't make Mama and Father our sacrificial lambs, especially only to spare our lives for the few days it will take them to catch up with us. Punishment for us all will be sure and swift. Trial by rifle."

The cracked walls of their single-room shelter seemed to hold their breath for them. They heard no sound except the occasional flutter of turkey wings from the fattening pen or the periodic churning of mud by one of the underfed swine. The clouds were thickening in fast smoky plumes on the outskirts of the village.

Just as the skies began to open up Father walked in from the fields, ahead of schedule, and tore off his muddied boots. His suspicion was immediately piqued by his sons' ashen stares. "What is it, my sons? You look as if there is something on your minds."

"No, Papa," Iwan quickly responded with a forced yet convincing smile. He shot Petro a remonstrative glance before his brother could cough up the truth. "We were just hoping that you made it back before the rains soaked you to the bone. How were the fields today, Father?"

Sunken yet dogged, Father replied, "We're down more men in the village. They say we may have lost another fifteen or twenty since last week. Thank God we got the garden planted when we had the help but I don't know how we're going to survive another winter if we don't have a good spring. Halyna has lost her two sons now and we'll have to help her. I don't know how we'll do it but I'm going to need you both now more than ever."

Halyna lived directly across the hall on the other side of the house from Iwan and Petro. Both Iwan and Petro knew that by *lost,* Father meant *in the regime.* Were Halyna's sons the ones forced to place Iwan and Petro's conscription notice on the door? If Iwan and Petro accepted the conscription how many doors would *they* be leaving notices on? How many lives would they be forced to ruin?

Mama trudged in shortly afterwards, her face a canvas for the cracks that work, worry, and ill nutrition had etched into her skin. But her figure was strong and looming—the way you'd expect a field slave's to look. She was stalwart and robust—her shoulders only slightly slumped from feeling the weight of the world, her frame only minimally more whittled than its age should have allowed.

After a quick greeting, Mama busied herself with the task of preparing dinner, dutifully turning beets into soup and wheat into bread. The boys relished the humming of life that gave them a fleeting glance of normalcy. As the shroud of parental love surrounded them, so, too, did the dread of the impending decision they were both too young to have to make.

Night came to the village and to the brothers but, naturally, sleep did not.

●

After the first light crept through the worn gauze curtains, the morning hours unfolded quickly. Although it was nearly May the fields had only recently begun their thaw. Winter's grasp was strong and the earth seemed to still be in the embrace of the dark season.

A teakettle boiled and again the familiar sounds of business as usual crept in. Mama was in the kitchen preparing breakfast to ready her husband and sons for a long day in the fields.

Father climbed into his layered gear. "Ahh, today won't be so bad, my sons. I hope the short rainfall was enough to loosen the fields a bit. If we get a move on this morning we may even be able to pull up some of the early radishes to take to market. I was thinking it might be nice to trade a little of it for some cured meats. You know, it may be time to start thinking of putting a few cans under the floorboards for safekeeping."

Iwan and Petro rolled over and caught each other's eyes. Locked in a silent battle of a million words the brothers' knowing glances moved towards tears but then veered away to resolution.

"Yes, Father," Iwan began, "let's get an early start. I think we've got enough potatoes and peas that we shouldn't have any problems trading for some salted pork. And," he added, casting a downward glance, "I think you're right. It's time to pack some food stores away."

"You know, boys," Father began, his voice barely audible, "I've got half a mind to join the resistance. I can't take any more news of our sons going to the Communist Army. What if you're next? What if they come knocking on our door?"

"But Father, joining the resistance is futile. More sure than the sun rising tomorrow will be your execution," Petro interjected. Then, perhaps testing the old man's sense of logic, maybe even looking for approval, but definitely before feeling the quick stab of his brother's eyes, he blurted out, "If they come for us, well, then, we'll go, Father."

"Dammit, Petro!" Father slammed his powerful fist down with such force that his slab of bread bounced off his plate and onto the floor. Immediately collecting himself, he slowly and deliberately picked the bread up off the dusty floor and continued, enunciating every syllable with the purposeful intent of regaining power, his voice grasping every word. "You. Will. NOT. Join..." There was a slight pause and with exaggerated disgust Father concluded his sentence. "Them."

Father looked at Petro and Iwan with severe consternation. "Have your heads been filled with the empty promises of their minions? I doubt they have because you are bright boys and we haven't seen any good come of this *wonderful* regime. They appear in the middle of the night and take our boys, children never to be seen again. They murder those that don't follow. Which is worse? To take your chances with the resistance or to live a life full of dishonor, forced to execute your way through town after town, leaving nothing behind but broken dreams, broken hearts, and a gibberish of promises no one has any intention of keeping?

"My heart fears for you, sons. It fears that the day will come when you are forced to make this decision for yourselves. I have lived on bended knee praying for the time when we could rise up and reclaim the right to our own lives! But it is clear that we live no more for ourselves. We will be led down the path of despair and disgrace only to find that our will is not our own."

Father paused long enough to acknowledge Mama's silent and still weeping. She sat stoically over her cup of tea, betrayed only by the tears streaming over the bridge of her nose.

"I will be damned if I turn on my country, if I agree to steal the souls of my brothers and sisters. And I will be damned if my sons will be taken by a dark cloud that will never be satisfied until it has rolled over and destroyed everything. Promise me you will not go. Promise me!" He slammed his fist down one more time and then quickly rose to add emphasis to his demand.

"Yes, Father," both boys dutifully responded. Knowing what they knew, it made it even harder not to give in to the innate desire to collapse in a heap of sorrow. But times like this made people who they were—not from the outside in, but rather, from their core. At this moment, the unspoken answer was clear. Iwan was right. Father was right. They must not join. Two lives in ruin were enough.

A moment later their door burst open and one of the village ladies ran in. She grabbed Mama by her skirt tail as she stood over the stove, eventually collapsing both women to their knees. "It's happened again! Daria, it's happened again!" Trembling, she continued, "I went to check on Halyna. She is gone. Gone! They took her. I told her sons they must go, but they did not." Sobbing, she fought hard to catch her breath. "Do you understand, Daria? They are going to take us all. I'm next. You're next." She tried to point a frail finger towards Iwan and Petro. "And so are they. I didn't think it would happen in our village but they are going to come for us all."

Father began to comfort both women but words would not escape his throat. Wrapping his arms around his wife and her friend, Father could only offer the fleeting comfort that his two strong, field-worked arms could provide. Again he tried to speak but his heart took control of his mind and his words were stifled. There was no comfort to offer. Helplessness sunk in like the cold grip of death.

Not knowing what to do, the boys also wrapped their arms around their Mama and her friend. Once the proud matriarchs of their families, the women's ever-sturdy figures collapsed in fear of the grim reaper's knock, a reaper carrying a red flag which bore a yellow sickle.

Father looked up at his sons and the trio of eyes locked in instant knowing. For the sake of all their lives, secrets had to be kept. Promises would be unrealistic. If Mama and Father knew for sure that their sons had been conscripted but did not go, retaliation would be certain and swift. Words would have to remain unspoken. Plans would be made. Hope and chance would be their only friend. For all of them, only one thing was certain. This life was dead.

Father was always fond of saying, *Today is a gift*. But not that today. That today was a tragedy. Yesterday, before the storm clouds brought despair, they had the ability to keep death at arm's length and pretend the sun would continue to shine over their village. Yesterday was the gift. And any tomorrows would be a miracle.

CHAPTER 2

The Others

Petro and Iwan's parents, Pavlo and Daria.
Photos courtesy of the Zapar family

The remaining populace became more submissive to the communist demands, and conscription into the Communist Army was easier. Anyone who refused, if caught, was shot. Iwan and Petro refused to report.

IT WAS MAY 5, 1931. Why or how the communists had not come for Iwan and Petro yet was anyone's guess. But the round up was coming. Two days had passed since they were to report and the low rumble among the villagers was that they, and several others, were marked for the firing squad. Fear and anxiety had turned the brothers' stomachs to the point that they could not eat, even though common sense told them they must. After that morning in the kitchen a curtain of solemnity fell over the family. Words were not spoken because there were no words. Knowing that a knock on the door could signify certain demise, the family did little more than go through the physical act of breathing. It was the only thing left that afforded them the feeling of existence.

Iwan and Petro could not ignore that their parents' usual standoffish demeanor—customary of that time and culture— softened a bit. Mama would hug them just a little bit longer and Father, when resting his arms on their shoulders, would pause and give a little squeeze. The whole family was par- alyzed—like chess pieces waiting to be played. But they could wait no longer.

That night, as the moon swept over the bristled treetops, the boys took the first steps into their new lives as fu- gitives—fugitives who were not on the run for something they did, but rather, simply by virtue of their mere existence during these hypocritical times, for something they didn't do. Quietly, so as not to wake Mama and Father, they si- lently inched their way into their clothes, careful to wear just enough layers to keep them warm but not so many as to hinder their flight.

They heard Mama roll over and they stopped mid-step. A few seconds later, things were silent again, so they crept to the front door. Petro slowly, almost as if not moving it at all, began to turn the knob. As they crept out into the spring frost they thought they heard the sound of their father rising from his bed. They couldn't afford to look back so they convinced themselves that the sound they'd heard was merely the wind. Hesitation could bring demise to the whole family, and they were all pawns now. The scent of last night's borscht still lingered in the air. The boys took one last breath of the comforting aroma and stole into the night.

At first they paused. They hadn't planned which way to go. They instinctively began to shuffle their feet to the west, towards the line of trees that marked the edge of their village. What started out as slow, non-committal steps quickly turned to deliberate pounding over composting leaves, jagged rocks, and wet grass. Over hills and past creeks the boys ran. They weren't paying attention to their heartbeats or their emotions or anything other than the distance they were putting between themselves and their home. Before they knew it they were at the edge of the forest and, as if by force, they both stopped at the same time, staring into the darkness and wondering what lay ahead.

They heard other footsteps nearby and their hearts beat out of their chests. Not saying a word, Iwan put out his hand and tightly grabbed his brother's shoulder. The stars in the sky were beginning to fade and the leading light of dawn gave off just enough of a glow for their eyes to catch a glimpse around them. That's when they saw the others. Boys, men—they were everywhere. And they all had the same look in their eyes as they headed towards the trees. Although purposeful in their stride, they shared a sense of panic. It could be felt permeating the air. They were all waiting for gunshots, terror, and death. But they all ran. They ran hopeful that they were rushing towards a life they could claim as theirs one day. They ran because running was all they had. Running meant they were alive...at least for tonight.

•

Back at the house, Father and Mama lay in bed. Mama wept and Father did his best to hold her while trying to hide the slow heaving of his own chest—for he was crying too. Silently, they said their prayers—in their hearts they said their goodbyes to Iwan and Petro. And they waited. The next day, they didn't get out of bed and were still holding each other when an officer and some guards representing the regime burst in looking for their sons. They told the truth—they didn't know where they were. Then they bent the truth a little in the hopes of lending their sons some time.

"They got a notice. They left. They're on their way to join your regime," Father said.

"*Tse Himno*! That's Bullshit!" the officer spat. "They were supposed to show up two days ago and never did. Where are you hiding them?"

"Search it," Father said, splaying his arms to the expanse of the room. Mama had wandered off to her familiar icon of the Virgin Mary with the baby Jesus and began whispering and pleading to them. Mama's fingers were bound in prayer so tightly they became white as she made the trembling form of the cross in front of her chest. One of the guards carelessly grabbed her and threw her to the floor. Papa rushed over to comfort her and they were spared a brief moment together.

The thud of shiny boots was all that they heard as the officer searched the premises for any trace of the boys. Smirking and satisfied that they were not there, he forced Mama and Father to stand, then edged them outside.

The familiar noises of cattle and poultry filled the air, but this time there was more. There was also the sound of quiet gasps, a heaving cry, anguished hearts, and sometimes shots—four or five at a time. Mama and Father kept their heads down but caught the glimpse of other bare feet out of the corners of their eyes. When they looked up they saw the others.

There was the town priest, the village doctor, the teacher, the chicken farmer. They were all there—even Halyna's friend. Too bereaved to look around anymore, they lowered their heads and continued waiting. There was little comfort to be had—other than the hope that their sons had each other and that they might find safety in numbers. As the sun rose in the skies their hearts wrenched in pain.

Soon the time came when wives were torn from their husbands, daughters from their fathers. As they were loaded onto the train cars bound for Siberia, Mama reached inside her shirt to cup her hands over the photo of her sons that she had stashed there, close to her heart.

On this day, the 5th of May, 1931, the parents of Iwan and Petro—Pavlo, just 51, and Daria, now 48—were sent off to serve ten years of hard labor in the Siberian labor camps as retaliation for embarrassing the communists. The family would never be reunited.

•

Not too many kilometers away, the boys ran. So steady was their pace that Iwan and Petro didn't even feel the pounding anymore—not the pounding of their feet or the pounding in their chests, not even the pounding of the shadows that ran alongside them as dawn turned to day. Trancelike, the boys ran deeper and deeper into the forest.

While initially concerned that some of the shadows might be those cast by undercover communists, their fear of the others quickly dissipated—common purpose provided a small sense of security. There *were* others. They weren't the only ones who had to make this decision. They weren't the only ones who had to leave behind everything they knew. And they weren't the only ones who had those haunting images playing in their heads of what would happen to their parents when the regime figured it all out. But still, comfort began to set in as they realized they were not alone. No words were spoken as they all continued to run. With no food and only the clothes on their backs they pushed ahead.

They were quickly approaching steep banks that plunged into a rushing river spanning about 400 meters...when they felt it. Dark clouds were closing in on them. They could hear the sounds of the whistles. They could hear dogs barking and shots in the distance. How far away were they? Petro and Iwan stopped dead in their tracks.

Petro's face lost all color and, struggling to catch his breath, he began to communicate with his brother in a sort of shouting whisper. "Iwan, what now? They are closing in on us. They can't be more than one, maybe two, minutes away. Quick brother, we need to hide!"

Iwan had a little vein that ran smack down the middle of his forehead. Always on an even keel in the days before the dark cloud, that little vein had barely been noticeable. But ever since the day they got the letter, it seemed to be on permanent high alert. Iwan's brow creased along that vein as he took a few seconds to survey the fields. To Petro it felt like an eternity.

Iwan turned to his brother and said, "Hiding is not an option. If we were going to hide, we would have stayed in the village."

Without further instruction Iwan started taking off his clothes—Petro followed suit. Quickly, but with purpose, the brothers tied their belts around the folded clothes and clamped the buckles down tight. Scared and nearly bare, they made a run for it.

On their heels were those sounds again. Except this time, the dogs were closing in. The shots were louder and accompanied by a whirring sound as they pierced the air in front and beside Iwan and Petro. They continued gathering speed so fast they felt weightless. Adrenaline had kicked in and they were in a full sprint. Faster and faster they ran, eyes forward. One misstep meant certain death. The urge to look backwards for the dark cloud was greater than they could imagine. The urge to look sideways for the others and the much needed comfort they might offer was something they simply couldn't afford.

They ran so fast that before they knew it they were looking straight down at the rumbling river below. They halted in their tracks. Some of the others had already dived in. Some were being swept downstream while others had just made it to the other side.

After a slight hesitation, Petro grabbed Iwan's hand and leapt. They plunged down over the muck of the banks and into the swollen river. Their first few strokes were frantic and erratic. But they felt each other's current and fell into a rhythmic cadence of power and speed. Iwan thought for a moment that the soldiers were throwing rocks at them but then he heard that piercing noise again and realized that the rifles were lined up on the banks, firing at close range.

The river quickly turned to death as the bullets shrilled into its waters and found their targets. The cadence of many of the others' strokes ebbed and the blood red waters swelled around them.

"He's still there. He's still there. He's still there," Iwan thought, in an internal meditative chant. As he struggled to stay both beside his brother and focused on the other side, Iwan fought off the feeling of doubt that they would get out of this alive.

As soon as their fingers touched the sweet mud of the far bank, Iwan and Petro heaved themselves and their belted clothing out of the water. They still had about five meters of almost straight vertical to climb before they could continue their escape. One half meter at a time the brothers scrambled up the bank. Digging their hands into the mud and clinging to whatever roots were buried underneath, then plunging their feet deep into the earth, they continued their torturous ascent.

Petro reached the top first and threw his stalwart frame into the mossy ground. Without a moment's hesitation he reached down for Iwan. As Iwan clasped his arm around his brother's and took a deep breath for his final pull, the earth shook right next to him and a bullet pierced the deep, soft mud close to the calf of his left leg. Almost as quickly as he realized what was happening, Petro hoisted him up so fast that they both tumbled over together onto the cold mucky bank.

Scrambling to their feet again, the brothers ran. The sounds of the shadows were still there but not as loud. There weren't nearly as many of the others as there had been when they had reached the edge of the river. Some had been shot, some had drowned, but some had made it. *They* had made it. And the deafening sound of the dark cloud had subsided. But still they ran. They ran so long and so far that dusk greeted them before their footsteps came to a halt.

Hungry and tired, the boys gave in to the need to sit down. The woods were still and quiet and darkness provided both the fear of the unknown and the cloak of invisibility. Falling to the ground in a dizzying heap, the boys finally stopped and caught their breath. When they did they looked at each other and, as if gazing into a mirror, they saw terror in the other's face. Their eyes burned with dust and pollen and, looking down at their hands, they realized their fingers and toes were bloodied and worn. Not one finger had the usual grooves of a fingerprint and their feet had been sliced like a garden after the plow horse had finished its job. Soon the stinging and soreness began to creep in.

Their clothes were beginning to dry in the May breeze and their muscles began to relax from their fear-induced grips. They found shelter under a jutting forest rock, and for the first time since they left their house yesterday morning, their bodies relented and they slept. Just before nodding off, Iwan reached up to pull his shirt a little tighter around himself to stave off the cold, then plunged his fingers between his shirt and undershirt. As he closed his eyes and drifted off to sleep, his hand squeezed around the only protection he had—the safety pin.

CHAPTER 3

1934, The Return

During the years 1931 through 1934, Iwan and Petro lived in Germany while Ukraine suffered the great Soviet-made famine of 1932-1933, known in Ukraine as the Holodomor, or Extermination by Hunger. Iwan and Petro's flight from communist death squads to Berlin, Germany was only relatively and temporarily safe. They evaded the black heart of communism only to find themselves in the midst of Hitler's build up of the Nazi war machine. They had escaped from communism but could see the developing hysteria which would in a few years precipitate World War II, and they wanted no part of Hitler's fanaticism either! Through veiled correspondence with hometown villagers in Pilna-Ternova, and after hearing word of the Holodomor, they felt compelled in 1934 to return to the village to determine their parents' status.

THE TWO BROTHERS did not suffer the fate of thousands of the Ukrainian people who were left behind. After the terrifying escape and that first night spent outrunning soldiers deep into the Carpathian mountainside, they continued their westward flight, surviving by whatever means necessary. Eventually they wound up in Berlin, Germany, nearly 900 kilometers from their village.

During their journey there, they had never granted themselves any false sense of security. City by city, village by village, they picked up odd jobs that offered them transit, shelter, or food. Sometimes they would blend in with field workers and sleep in barns after a day of hard labor and sometimes they would help load and unload trains, saving their money to later exchange for tickets that would take them further west.

In this new life of exile, they simply existed. Remnants of what they had seen that night were etched in their memories. That, along with the disheartening rumors of village devastation and the feeling of being hunted, kept them away from their tiny village of Pilna-Ternava for the next three years.

Every day, despair greeted them. But every day, they continued to wake up from their beds of hay, grass, or, oftentimes, simply dirt, and go about the business of their new lives—lives of emancipated imprisonment. Although they wandered under their own volition, they were not yet truly free.

Unfortunately, they were only relatively safe in Berlin. By 1934, they found themselves in the midst of Hitler's rapidly developing Nazi hysteria that was about to precipitate World War II. They wanted no part of Hitler's fanaticism and they knew that their safety would be increasingly jeopardized.

Through veiled correspondence with a few of the others, Petro and Iwan decided they must return to their village one last time. Not a day passed that they didn't think about their parents—as they lay under the stars they would often wonder if Father and Mama were down here wondering about them, or up in the Heavens guiding them.

•

On one such evening, nearly three years to the day from when they left, Iwan's piercing dark brown eyes were scanning the spring clouds. The air was beginning to warm and the smell of lilacs on the soft breeze gave him an almost defiant feeling in the pit of his stomach. He closed his eyes and lingered on the perfumed breeze as the blue hour of dusk started closing in. Inches away he could see his older brother's chest rising and falling with the rhythmic sound of the cicadas.

After an unnaturally long inhale, as if to preface his words with an exclamation point, Iwan let out a slow and deliberate exhale. "It's time."

Petro rolled over to his side, so desperate to rest his tired muscles after having unloaded boxcars since dawn that he couldn't even muster any words or expression.

"Petro, did you hear me? It's time. We have to go back."

Hanging on to the deliberateness of his brother's statement, Petro slowly sat straight up so that he could look his brother in the eyes.

"What makes you so sure, Iwan?"

"Nothing makes me so sure, brother. Nothing ever could. But we've got to know. If Mama and Father are dead, we need to honor them. If, by the grace of God they are alive, we need to find them. The monotony of living as if we are all dead is going to rot us alive." He reached into the satchel and pulled out a small leather pouch they used to hold their savings. "I've counted it four times already. I think we've got what we need to get back. We'll leave tomorrow."

And so began the eastward trek back to their homeland—full of renewed hope, familiar despair, and unsettling trepidation.

•

The first thing that struck them as they neared the edge of the village forest was the stillness. It was just past dusk and the usual stirrings of cattle and poultry were few and far between. Occasionally they could hear wagon wheels mucking up the dusty lane or the sound of the slop bucket being tossed out to the fields before the lady of the house turned back in and shut the door.

Although this relative quiet was unfamiliar, it was comforting in comparison to the sounds that had crept back into their heads—the sounds of bullets whizzing by, the painful wails, and the bark of the enemy.

Iwan shuttered as if to shake off the past. Side by side, he and Petro stared into the distance at their village—straight down the dusty lane and a little to the right past the line of evergreens there was an island of trees that surrounded where their house, and their parents, should be. They sat this way for hours not entirely sure of what to do, hoping to see a familiar and trusting face.

As dusk gave way to the pitch dark of night they saw one of their old neighbors stumble out of his barn towards his home. With no other soul in sight, and remembering the overheard secretive talks of resistance between the old man and their father, they knew this was their chance.

"Mr. Shevchenko," Iwan said in a voice raised just over a whisper. "Mr. Shevchenko!"

The old man looked in the direction of the woods—Petro grabbed a rock and tossed it towards him, calling the old man's name one more time.

Mr. Shevchenko started back towards his house but abruptly turned on his heels and began walking towards them. As he got closer the boys could see his frail frame and the cracks of worry on his face. His dogged eyes struggled to pierce through the darkness to see who was summoning him. As he got closer a strange mix of fear and exhilaration crept across his face.

"Iwan? Petro? Is that you, boys?"

"Yes, Mr Shevchenko. We've come back for Mama and Father. Are they here?" Petro stammered.

"Oh, my sons," Mr. Shevchenko said, deflated. "Where have you been? It's been so long since that night when they took them away. Half of our village is dead and the other half has been sent to Siberia. We did what we were told and for what? This?" He looked over his shoulder at the stark, eerie scene that lay before them. It was a ghost town. No cattle brayed, no neighbors stood along the stoops to converse—just dust and weeds lining the solemn streets.

"My son is gone. He's one of *them* now," Mr. Shevchenko said with scorn. "And again, for what? So we could give them everything we had? Our homes, our land, our food? This world is broken and it's not possible that we can fix it. You can't fix it either. You need to leave. There is nothing here for you. You have the gift of youth. Use it."

"But, Mr. Shevchenko," started Iwan, "we must know. Mama and Father. Where are they? Siberia? Or worse?"

"It's hard to say which is worse, boys. Don't put unrealistic thoughts in your head or they will just make life harder than it already is for us all. You must know...either was a death sentence." His voice trailed off but then lifted a bit. "But I did see them that day."

His eyes drifted as if watching a newsreel. "I knew by the look in your father's eyes as they herded them out of the village with the others that you two had gone. The curious thing was, as I was looking at them, all I could feel in myself was shame. Shame that I let my son be a part of this force that was taking life and extinguishing it with no more care than a farmer thinning his fields.

"It's true we were spared from the camps that night. But our lives were not ours. Our souls still belonged to them. They came back for our crops. There was so much death that bodies lay on the side of the road—too many to bury. We did what we could to honor them. Newborn children frail from disease and hunger because our mothers couldn't produce proper milk, being so emaciated themselves. Our livestock was taken and survival was without dignity, without duty to others. It was every person for himself. And it was hell. I lost my wife. First my son and then my wife. The sun rises and sets and it's not a new day. It's the same day. Lived over and over again in my mind.

"But Iwan, Petro...I will tell you this—that night, your father and I locked eyes. And I really can't explain it but I can tell you that it wasn't fear that I saw in those eyes. It was sadness, yes, but not fear. But more than that, it was hope. Hope for the both of you...and here you are. Proof that somewhere, in this twisted world that has become perverse with bloodshed, there is goodness. You are goodness."

With that, the old man fell to his knees on the soft leaves and wept quietly in the arms of the boys. And just as they had comforted Halyna's friend the night she came to Mother, they wrapped their arms around Mr. Shevchenko and silently wept with him.

As quickly as he had fallen to his knees, Mr. Shevchenko loosened his grip and rose up, sweeping the tears from his thin face. "You must leave—and don't return. There is nothing here for you. There are too many who will seek justice for their own by using you. Look at me and please understand that whether or not you went to the Communist Army, your parents would have faced a death sentence—whether by execution, slave labor, or forced starvation. But have peace in knowing that you are free. That is what they prayed for. That is what they wanted for you. I wish the same had been possible for my son. I just pray he is alive. Your parents are in Siberia. May they one day be free. May you one day be reunited. But until that day comes, be the hope that I saw on your father's face. Now go. And don't ever speak of seeing me and I won't ever speak of seeing you."

Then, the old man reached down to the earth and pulled up two stones. He presented one to each of the boys. "This is no longer your home, but you will always be, and always have, a part of this village. Take with you the hope of your father and mother, and the hope of all of us. It's all you've got. And you're all we've got."

With that, Mr. Shevchenko turned towards home. Iwan and Petro could sense that he yearned to say more or to turn around, but he continued down the lane until all they could see again was darkness.

Now, holding the answer to the question that had plagued them for the past three years, they knew there was one more thing they had to do as the night continued to deepen.

They crept down the path, careful not to throw shadows where they could be seen. They moved down the dusty lane, to the line of trees, and a little to the right. They saw what was their house, but through the curtains the faint glow of candlelight revealed a young couple at the dinner table—the same table they used to sit around. Frail and thinning, the wife sat across from her husband as they shelled some May peas into the very same pot that Mama had used. A brief sense of sorrow gave way to a glimmer of resolve as the boys slowly turned back around and made their way out of the village. They were relieved that this time they were granted the solitude of their thoughts.

CHAPTER 4

Love and War

Daria Krushews'kyi from Krywen'ke, Ukraine.
Photo courtesy of the Zapar family.

Since Iwan & Petro couldn't help their parents in any way except to pray for their survival, they chose to stay with and work for a friend of their family, Sergiy Chervoniy, who lived in a town called Kotsiubintsi. This friend ran a small general store and said he could use help running it so he hired the brothers. Iwan & Petro had such a keen business sense that after a short time the friend suggested they open their own store since the town was large enough to support two stores. So they did, and the brothers ran it successfully.

RUNNING THE GENERAL store really wasn't so different from the day-to-day trading that Iwan and Petro did with Father when they took their vegetables to market. As it turned out, Iwan and Petro had a keen business sense. Maybe it was due to the need to turn a profit in order to sustain even their simple lifestyle, or maybe it was innate, but before long their little store was flourishing.

After their equivocal tvisit home, the boys became resolute in their need to find some semblance of normalcy. They quickly fell into the rhythm of their new lives and the noose of worry began to lessen...if only slightly. Their hard work and the resulting success of their bustling business afforded them the ability to rent a room a stone's throw away from their shop.

One warm summer afternoon Iwan was busying himself behind the counter, tallying the day's receipts. The screen door was open to let in the breeze and Petro was sweeping the splintered wood planks. It was almost a picture perfect day—a breeze blew in from down the lane, a breeze laced with the sweet smell of the canola fields.

Petro stopped his methodical sweeping when he heard the crunch of gravel outside. The footsteps drew near and brought a familiar face into the store. A genuinely wide grin appeared on Petro's face when he saw his now old friend, Sergiy. "Sergiy! Come sit down. It's been too long."

Iwan quickly brought the shop stool outside and Sergiy sat down. The boys were so appreciative of Sergiy's generosity and they were always happy when he was able to come for one of his visits. They loved to talk business with him and craved the good fortune of his patriarchal knowledge. Sometimes, it gave them a twinge of pain and guilt that made them miss their own father, but there was no denying that Sergiy's presence was also comforting.

Sergiy walked with a cane and had a slight stoop to his back—rounded by time spent over inventory sheets and balancing the till. But every Thursday he would walk down the lane to visit with the brothers.

Sergiy and the boys quickly fell into their routine conversation, discussing crops, weather, and war—usually in that order. When they had exhausted all the familiar topics, Petro got up to offer Sergiy some bread with honey and a glass of water. As he was turning to open the screen door, Sergiy grabbed him by the elbow. Iwan quickly turned around.

"Iwan. Petro. You boys are working so hard. Look at this store," he said, surveying what they had built. I'm as proud of you as if I were your own father. Nothing in your life has been easy. This I know. But you two are hard workers and smart, and most importantly you are deserving. I just can't help but think that, perhaps, there is something missing. You know, the scent of a woman, the thrill of young love...the cup of a nice, robust bosom." Sergiy closed his eyes and began cupping imaginary breasts—with that the boys broke into laughter.

Iwan, shaking his head, ran into the shop and quickly returned with a full bottle of vodka. Petro and Sergiy were still cracking each other up, conjuring imaginary breasts and hips in the warm breeze, when Sergiy turned his attention to Iwan.

"Iwan, you keep mentioning that you could use a little help with the store. And you've said before that you would consider marriage if the right woman were to come along. Well I think I may have just the right woman for you. Her name is Daria. Daria Krushews'kyi. Her father, Stephan, owns a store in Krywen'ke, about two hours from here. I've got to go next week to barter some of my fall seed for some of his coffee supply. Come with me."

"I don't know," Iwan wavered.

"What's the worst that could happen?" Sergiy continued cajoling him. "You leave Petro in charge of the store and you get one day to see a different village?"

Iwan looked reluctant but Petro piped in, "Brother, it's time. I see that look in your eyes when a family walks in here. I see how you stare at some of the ladies in the village. You pine for love. Me, well, I'm not quite ready to settle down with one woman just yet," he said with a wink. Petro enjoyed the ladies and a serious relationship would only get in the way of his spontaneous nature. His life on the run, going from town to town, had sculpted him into a true nomad. Almost as if by choice, an irrational fear of stability had grown within him. Not to mention that deep down, Petro was petrified to bring children into a world full of suffering and heartache.

Sergiy didn't wait for Iwan to respond. "Twelve o'clock next Thursday. I'll pick you up. And shave that face, just in case."

Iwan reached up and realized that it had been a couple days since he last remembered to shave. Instantly he was nervous. But he had seven days to contain his anxiety. His world consisted of work and worry. He wasn't sure that he could take on more than that.

They offered Sergiy *one more for the horse,* as they were wont to say, clinking their shot glasses together. Sergiy drank, then shakily leapt upon his nag, grabbed the reigns, and headed home.

•

"Petro, are you sure you've got all you need for the shop today? You know, I really don't mind staying here. It's not like Sergiy needs me to go with him. If you want me to I can stay."

Petro shook his head and gave a little smirk. Then he laughed under his breath and started in on his brother. "Iwan, for the love of Christ, go! You can't work your whole life away to punish yourself for our escape, depriving yourself of what may make you happy in the process. Mother and Father would want you to meet someone. I want it."

He reached up and flipped the collar of his brother's shirt down, ran his hands through Iwan's hair, and then grabbed him by the shoulders. Looking him straight in the eye, he spoke kindly but firmly. "Brother, go find your happiness. Sergiy may be leading you straight to it. Or maybe not. But at the very least you will be out of this store, away from me for the day, and seeing more than these four walls. You deserve it. I'll be okay."

Iwan gave his brother a smile and then pushed off his shoulders with a quick slap and the hint of a smile. He busied himself in the store a few moments more, going over the day's expected deliveries with Petro. Then Sergiy pulled his wagon to the side of the dusty road and gave a quick whistle. At that, Iwan bounded down the steps and hopped up onto the wooden bench seat right next to Sergiy. For the first time in years his cheeks were flushed with excitement. As the warm breeze tousled his hair, Iwan eased back into the seat and gave in to whatever lay ahead.

•

Iwan and Sergiy pulled into the village of Krywen'ke around noon. They made their way through the narrow lane and past the wooden fences, the wandering livestock, and the farmers coming home with a few fruits and vegetables from the fields for their lunch. Wives were in the kitchen with kids tugging at their aprons and warm loaves of bread were rising in the ovens.

As the wagon settled to a stop, Iwan's pulse quickened and he could feel sweat beading up on his brow. He grabbed his handkerchief out of his pocket and wiped it away, then settled into step with Sergiy as they strolled up the path to the house.

The door swung open and two little girls in traditional Ukrainian attire greeted them at the walkway happily inviting them inside. Iwan couldn't help but smile and felt a little more at ease as they walked into the house.

The first thing he noticed was the smell of food. Not just any smell, but the Heavenly aroma of home cooked sausages, varennyky, steaming borscht, and a home baked torte. It felt like home, and family, and all the smells he thought he would never remember. But here they were—those familiar scents lingering in the air, enveloping him in an instant sense of security and belonging. His eyes scanned the house looking for clues as to who may live here. Right then he heard the shuffling of shoes coming around the corner.

Iwan looked at the ground and watched the slippers appear. He looked up—there stood Daria. She was well under five feet tall but as she began choreographing the layout of the meal, she projected a much taller image. Her olive skin and dark, well-coifed hair made her look older than her shy smile and naïve eyes indicated. It was instantly apparent that Iwan was intrigued by her. He could tell that, even by the standards of the era, Daria was a take-charge kind of girl—and he couldn't take his eyes off of her.

"Iwan," Sergiy began, "I am pleased to introduce you to my old friend, Stefan, and his wife, Maria. And here is his beautiful daughter, Daria."

"Pleased to meet you, Stefan." Iwan shook Stefan's hand, nodded and smiled at Maria, then went over to Daria. Their eyes locked and he did a shy little bow of his head. Then he tried to look anywhere other than at her incredibly plump bosom modestly covered by her sheer embroidered blouse.

Fortunately for him, the vodka bottle came out immediately and they all took a seat. The aroma of the meal was enough of a distraction to prevent himself from fulfilling his need to pour over every inch of Daria with his eyes.

There was an unimaginable amount of food at the table— Iwan had never really seen such a spread in his life. Instantly thinking of Petro, he couldn't help but hope that they would send him home with a basket of leftovers so that Petro could enjoy it, too.

Stefan sat at the head of the table right next to Sergiy. Iwan awkwardly pulled the seat out next to him for Daria to sit down. She smiled and nodded nonchalantly and then expertly went about the business of helping her mother pass the plates around the table.

Iwan tried to keep up as the plates slid by him —more kept coming from the kitchen. Toast after toast and plate after plate, Iwan did his best to mind his manners and keep sampling. But life on the run for so long had accustomed his stomach to meager portions. He was wont to reach his limits after little sustenance, and he quickly filled up.

The vodka was flowing and Iwan was starting to feel his cheeks flush even more than he thought possible. His head was getting a little cloudy, but he could feel himself relaxing, too. Stefan, Sergiy, and Iwan chatted about politics and the store—Iwan tried to offer up some sage-sounding business advice he had acquired along the way.

Perhaps Iwan's eyes were a little too relaxed—he began to survey the guests at the table and take advantage of those brief seconds when he had enough time to envision Daria's naked bosom through the soft folds of her frock. He was smitten.

Daria felt it, too. At one moment, as she walked into the room from the kitchen, she pretended to busy herself with scanning the crowd of guests. But from the corner of her eye she could feel Iwan staring at her. And she could feel in that stare that Iwan liked what he saw. Being from such a small village she didn't really know how to act around men but in her gut she could feel that Iwan was intrigued by her—this gave her confidence. Her nerve grew by the minute and she soon realized that if he were to speak directly to her she would be able to find the words to converse with him.

Daria grew genuinely interested in Iwan and, before the third shot of vodka made its way around the table, she began doting on him. Was some sort of universal guidance or fate at work? The air was electric. She was falling for Iwan, fully reciprocating his fantasies. Her eyes followed the angular lines of his face and, when he wasn't looking, they would rest on his strong, well-chiseled arms and broad, sculpted chest. Daria could see that Iwan was no stranger to hard work and when her eyes caught his, she got butterflies in her stomach.

She instantly felt a sense of security and ease when Iwan spoke. And in a world that had become full of ups and downs and twists of fate, she sensed an even keel in Iwan's demeanor. Daria's take-charge attitude sometimes got in the way of her own patience and levelheadedness, and something about Iwan felt like a good balance for her. Yes, already, he felt like a good fit. Daria was only fifteen but, having seen the suffering on the faces of so many of her family members these past few years, Daria knew a strong man was her best chance to get out of her little village.

She hardly noticed her straying thoughts as the meal dwindled to a close. The men, bloated from the heavy fare and lazy from the vodka, reconvened out in the front yard under the chestnut tree to continue their conversation. The women, all small in stature, stooped over the wash bin to begin the chore of hand cleaning the multitude of dishes. Daria hurriedly fulfilled her part of the washing and ran to her room to freshen up. Then she wandered as nonchalantly as possible out to the front yard to commandeer Iwan.

"Iwan, would you like for me to show you around our village?" Daria asked.

Iwan needed to stretch his legs before the long ride back to Petro so he quickly obliged. But he would have gone with her even if he were preparing to walk back home. The two wended their way through the fields, down the dusty roads, past curious neighbors peeking out from their gates at the striking stranger walking around with Daria. Daria proudly strolled Iwan past the houses, expertly playing the line between the innocent girl that she was and the blossoming woman she would soon become.

Iwan instantly liked Daria and could tell that she had a keen sensibility and an intellect well beyond that of a fifteen-year-old girl from a small village. She wasn't like some of the girls that he and Petro had come across in their travels. She wasn't silly or flashy. She seemed genuine and real and Iwan began to feel something that he had never really experienced before. He began to feel the first grasp of love's warm hand.

Daria strolled at his side for most of the walk, her arms clasped behind her back in a purposeful kind of way. He was trying to hang on her every word but couldn't help his wandering mind as his eyes gazed upon her stout legs and feminine curves. For a young girl from a remote village she was well put together.

The only awkwardness between them was the fact that Iwan didn't feel comfortable talking about himself. He was more interested in finding out about her than he was in sharing anything about his life. The initial moments of their conversation seemed a bit forced, but Daria had an uncanny way of pushing the conversation and forcing him to talk.

"Dammit, Iwan!" he thought to himself. He wanted to keep a wall up to distance himself from any more disappointment, or worse, loss. For the past few years both Iwan and Petro had lived by the tacit motto that you can't lose what you don't have. Plus, he felt unspectacular. What was he going to talk about that would impress this beautiful girl? What about this life of his could possibly make her want to leave her village and be with him? Insecurity was beginning to sink in, as it always did, but fortunately for Iwan, Daria wasn't going to let Iwan's wall of mystery and self doubt remain standing.

They strolled a little further and ended up down by a mountain stream. Laughing playfully, Daria grabbed Iwan by his hand and pulled him down to sit with her. They both took off their shoes and plunged their toes into the cold water below. It felt good to Iwan. It had been quite some time since he was this carefree. The vodka helped a little, too.

Daria pulled up her dress a little higher exposing just a bit of her thighs and Iwan couldn't resist the urge to grab her hand and pull her closer to him. He felt that burning and, giggling nervously, the two locked eyes as Iwan tenderly placed his lips to hers. Daria edged closer to him, brushing her fingertips up and down the length of his tight arms then down his spine until they finally rested softly around the linen that clung to his buttocks.

She felt she couldn't resist but just as quickly her shy side took over and she pulled away. In the sunlight, the two froze—neither quite sure what to do next other than issue a couple of nervous giggles. They sat and talked by the bank for a few more minutes until they could hear the call of one of the pesky roosters and what sounded like someone coming through the woods towards them. Jumping up, they grabbed their shoes and Daria pulled Iwan by the arm all the way back to where the rest of the crew sat anxiously awaiting their return.

Iwan's damp trouser legs and Daria's ear-to-ear smile were not overlooked by those they'd left back at the house. Iwan caught Sergiy's stare and saw the beginning of a smile just as he looked away to disguise the red creeping up to his cheeks and ears.

With his much-hoped-for plateful of leftovers for Petro in hand, it was time for Iwan and Sergiy to head back home. Sergiy climbed up on the wagon first, giving Iwan a chance to say a proper good bye to Daria.

"Daria, I had fun down at the river with you today. I'm wondering if maybe I could see you again soon?"

Daria blushed slightly. "Me, too. It was nice to sneak away for a few minutes with you. Let's do that again soon. You know where to find me," she said with a coy smile.

Iwan grabbed her hand and slowly planted a tender kiss on top of it. "Yes, let's make that happen. I'll be back soon. While I'm gone, be looking for another spot where we can run off to." With that, he gave a polite nod and a quick smile and then jumped up to his seat alongside Sergiy.

As the wagon wheels slowly turned, Sergiy reached over, patted Iwan on the leg, gave a sly little wink and said, "I told you it was time."

Steady ahead, the two friends started for home. For the first time since running the fields with Petro and speaking their *Talabarske*, Iwan felt untroubled and carefree. He could feel himself giving into the whims of love and wishing his time with Daria hadn't passed so quickly.

•

The following Thursday, Iwan went with Sergiy back to Krywen'ke and back to Daria. He continued to do so every Thursday for nearly a year. Each week, Sergiy would talk about world events with Stefan and Maria while Daria and Iwan stole some quiet moments down by the water, exploring each other—both physically and mentally. It was such an innocent time for Daria and Iwan, and a time of complete and utter happiness and anticipation. In between visits the inseparable bond between the two lovers continued to grow, as each would count down the days until the next visit. When they were apart, neither could stop thinking about the other or the promise of their next visit together.

•

Even for the time, Daria was a strong-headed girl who spoke her mind and often led the rest of the family in their day-to-day operations. She was wise beyond her years, an old soul who seemed to know what to expect at every turn and quite adept at keeping her family in line. In her mind she was rarely wrong about her staunch opinions but, curiously enough, when she met Iwan, she relished the chance to let go of the reins, or at least to loosen her grip. For lack of a better phrase, she had met her match.

Often, while the two were either finished with or shirking their chores and duties, they would talk about the state of the world, religion, politics. Iwan had a way of leading Daria with a gentle strength and even though she felt some of her control weakening, she slowly began to willingly relinquish it...along with her heart. When he was with her, she felt complete and happy and carefree. When he left, she started to keep a journal so she wouldn't forget to tell him anything he may have missed when he came back the next week.

Every time she thought of Iwan her heart burned for the next time she would see him—when they could steal away under the leggy pines. And just the thought of his smiling face visible in the distance over the reins of the horse made her body ache for his touch.

Iwan enjoyed having a sense of family again and accepted the oft-given fatherly advice of Stefan. The more he got to know the fellow the more he liked him. Like Iwan and Petro, Stefan had not had an easy life.

At the time, Stefan was about 46. In his younger days, when World War I broke out, Stefan was conscripted into the Austrian army and was sent into battle. He never spoke about what he saw during the war, but he came home with a bullet wound to his head that left him without his left eye. Its socket was now concealed under a patch, and he had very restricted use of his left arm. He was discharged and received a pension, but the pension was so small he had to find work to sustain his growing family. He originally operated farming equipment and plowed the fields of Krywen'ke, but his physical limitations proved to be too much so he opened his now thriving general store in the heart of their village.

Daria's mother was a role model for her. Iwan keenly watched the way the two interacted to imagine what kind of wife and mother Daria would be. Iwan was more than pleased with what he saw.

Since Maria and Stefan had two other children—a son, Roman, and a daughter, Olga, who were both younger than Daria, Iwan felt confident that Maria would be able to run the household with their assistance. Reassuring himself with this knowledge, and with great hope and excitement, Iwan decided that it was time for Daria to join him in forming their own household. He looked forward to being with Daria fulltime and to managing a thriving family of their own.

•

Finally, on November 24, 1936, after nearly a year of courting both Daria and her family, Iwan proposed marriage. At first, Stefan was hesitant to give his daughter's hand in marriage, merely for the reason that he felt Daria was too young at the age of sixteen, but he recognized their love for each other and knew that Iwan was a good man.

So the two married in a little chapel in the quiet village of Krywen'ke. There was no fanfare in the traditional sense, but the affection between Daria and Iwan was so apparent that a good majority of the village turned out to bless their young love. The village church was garnished with berries and fresh cut wheat from the fields and Daria was adorned with traditional Ukrainian ribbons and a bouquet of flowers as she walked down the aisle to her dear Iwan.

And, of course, Petro proudly stood by the side of his brother. He was glowing with love and admiration for his newfound extended family nearly as much as Iwan was.

**Daria and Iwan on their wedding day.
Photo courtesy of the Zapar family.**

As Daria and Iwan betrothed themselves to each other in the hazy sunshine of a late fall afternoon, they felt apprehensive not about the love they shared for one another, but about what lay ahead. But they cast aside all of those thoughts and enjoyed the seemingly endless days–long celebration amongst all of those they loved.

Even as Iwan stood before the villagers offering his vows, he imagined Mama and Father standing with him, smiling at his beautiful bride. A couple of times he reached inside his coat pocket to feel for Mama's safety pin, desperately wanting her to be there with him, and somehow knowing that she was.

Deep into the last night of their wedding celebration Iwan and Daria led the village feast and accepted an immeasurable number of toasts—to love, to marriage, to life—until finally, they gave themselves to each other not as mere lovers but as betrothed husband and wife. Then they gave in to the weight of their exhaustion and fell asleep in each other's arms.

CHAPTER 5

The Burning

Daria's mother, Maria, had passed away of uterine cancer in 1940 and, by 1944, with the German army defeated by Russia at the Battle of Stalingrad, the remaining German forces were in full retreat through westward Ukraine. As most armies do in a retreat, the German army burned everything in their path, and the village of Krywen'ke was on full alert that the Germans were headed their way.

AFTER THEY SETTLED into married life, Iwan and Daria didn't have any plans to stray far. They enjoyed living with Stefan and Maria and helping in their general store.

A little over a year later, their first son, Lesio, was born. He was followed two years later by the birth of his brother, Lyiubchyk. Petro continued to run the store in the next town and Daria's family's store began to thrive as a result of Iwan's entrepreneurial spirit.

It was now 1940 and this period in the brothers' lives was the one they would look back on later and consider *normal.* But times change, and peace isn't always easy to come by.

●

One early afternoon Iwan was tending to the general store— stocking the shelves and going about his day—when Petro walked through the door. While it wasn't unusual for him to stop by from time to time during the week, especially to bring his nephews a treat from Uncle Petro, it was unusual that he was stopping by during the time he would typically be working in his own store. Iwan glanced up, trying to disguise his surprise, and said, "Brother! To what do I owe this pleasure today?"

Petro wore a very grave look on his face and his gauzy shirt looked dirty and disheveled—most likely from the dust his horses had kicked up as they sped down the dusty village road to bring Petro to his brother.

"Iwan, you're not going to believe this. Remember when we went home and spoke with Mr. Schevchynko?"

"Yes, Petro. Of course I do." He glanced down at Petro's coarse hands and saw that he was holding what looked to be a newspaper of some sort. Now his interest and concern was piqued.

"Well, if there was a doubt as to whether or not we could return to our beloved home village one day, I can now assure you, with great certainty, that we cannot. Ever." Petro's great sadness was masked by an even greater fortitude through which only a brother could see.

"Let me take a look, Petro. What are you talking about?" Iwan stretched out his hand towards the newspaper.

"Let's go inside, Iwan." Petro pulled the paper into his hip as if to hide it, then motioned towards the screen door. Glancing over his shoulder, Petro led his brother into the relative privacy of the store.

Remaining silent, Petro and Iwan stood against the counter and Petro began to unfold the newspaper. Iwan immediately recognized it as the paper from the village where they had grown up, the village they fled that terrible night. Instantly, a river of emotions welled up within his gut. His eyes struggled to make sense of the headlines. He didn't have to play this game long because instantly his eyes locked on the bottom left hand corner of the second page and he saw his own familiar face staring back at him. Right next to his own photo was his brother's. They were younger, much younger, but it was apparent that the two faces staring back at them were their own.

Astonished, Iwan's eyes darted from his photo to his brother's and then, as a flurry of emotions struck him, he scanned the surrounding words and made out *Zapar Brothers* and *traitors* and *Communist Army*. Not that they were the only ones listed under such headlines—the newspaper seemed to contain the communists' most wanted list—those to be hunted down at any cost.

Petro, unable to endure another moment of his brother's silence and utter astonishment, started in. "Brother, I know that we both knew it was unlikely that we could ever go back to our village. But now, as this war is churning and the struggle between the communists and the Nazis is ramping up even more, it's time for us both to think about what is next for us. For your family. We are not safe here in Ukraine. Previously, we thought we were just not safe in our village but now our capture is imminent—*They* haven't forgotten. They are looking for us. This showed up yesterday morning laying on a stack of firewood next to the store. Thank God I found it and glanced through it. I have no clue as to who risked their own life to warn us about ours but we must heed the warning. I don't think we need to pack up and leave today but, please, keep it in the back of your mind that as this war escalates, so too does the threat to our lives and the threat to those we have brought with us into this tangled web."

"Understood," muttered Iwan. "Loud and clear. We are not safe anywhere here. As much as I love Ukraine, any village we may find ourselves in will only ever serve as a place of temporary respite. We need real safety. Not just for us but for my wife and children. Not just for now but for the remainder of our days. I don't think there's a clear-cut road ahead of us but we must begin to forge a path away from the roots we have put down, the ones I selfishly longed for."

Iwan's eyes looked troubled beyond his years. He knew, yet again, that they would need to blaze a path out of a village that served as their home, away from their stable lives. They'd soon be back on the winding trail of the unknown. And Iwan also knew that it would mean saying goodbye and never returning to Daria's father, and all that he and Daria had built together these past few years.

"But, brother," Iwan began, "I'm not quite ready. I don't think it's time yet. You have my word that I understand. Fully. But please honor me with the gift of time. I need to make sure that we are leaving Stefan in a position of safety. And I need to give Daria and the boys some more time. I want Liubchyck and Lesio to be old enough so that, even though it may be fogged by their youth, they have a good recollection of their grandfather. Will you trust me on the timing?"

"Yes, brother, of course. You have many more people to say goodbye to than I do. I completely understand. Just remain vigilant and do what you must to give yourself peace of mind when the time comes. And I must ask that you promise me one more thing...and I will promise the same to you."

"What's that?" Iwan asked, raising an eyebrow in query.

While deliberately staring straight into his brother's dark eyes, Petro said, "Promise me that once we get out of Ukraine you'll know better than to ever return. It will be hard because, again, you have much more you are leaving behind. As long as the communists are in power we will never be safe here. And while we are here we are nothing more than human ghosts already marked for the rifle. You *must* never return under such conditions."

Iwan reached up and pulled his brother tightly to his chest. With a deep sigh, he whispered into his brother's ear, "Yes, Petro. As long as you promise me the same, we will be bound by that same promise. And I will always be bound to you."

With that, Petro walked over to the burning fireplace and tossed the newspaper into the fire.

•

With world events churning and news spreading of German retreat through Ukraine, Stefan and Iwan began the task of preparing for the grave prospects that lay ahead.

Stefan announced to Iwan one morning, "Son, it's time we prepare. The Germans are closing in on our little village and we are fools to think we may be spared. I know that you and Petro know this feeling all too well, but there may be nothing left once they get here."

Iwan, grateful once more for the guidance of an elder, agreed and so began the task of digging a hidden bunker as the starting point to their plan for safety. Together the men decided that the best spot would be under the stump of a once-hearty chestnut tree, just across a dirt path from their house. As they dug, there were other families around them doing the very same thing. By day, Krywen'ke came to life as the sounds of shovels and rolling wheelbarrows saddled with dried and salted foods filled the air. Neighbors negotiated over which trees would shelter each family, should the looming chaos ensue.

•

It was now early March, 1944. One afternoon, Daria set about the task of baking as Lesio and Lyiubchyk clung to her apron. Iwan and Stefan were in the store tending to inventory and sweeping up—readying the shop for closing. The late afternoon sun was peeking through the crack in the door and the spring breeze still carried the last chill of winter. Up until then the day was ordinary.

As Iwan was leaning on the counter, pencil in hand, counting the till, he noticed the sharp lead tip softly vibrate on the paper. Wide eyed and paralyzed, he froze in fear. He heard the sounds of cannons and gunshots off in the distance. After a few moments he could tell they were getting closer. The familiar sounds of battle rang in Iwan's ears and his heartbeat hastened.

Iwan, Stefan, and Petro looked up at each other and spun around in their tracks, bolting for the door. Iwan bounded up the stairs to grab Daria and the boys.

"Daria! We've got to go—now!" Iwan yelled. Daria didn't hesitate. By the look of terror in Iwan's eyes, she knew this was a grave decision he had been forced to make in a fraction of a second. She quickly ran to get some blankets and pillows.

Just as she opened a dresser drawer to pile in some clothes, Petro grabbed her arm and guided her out of the house as quickly as he could. Iwan had Lyiubchyk cradled in his arms and Petro had Lesio. The scene was the same everywhere throughout the village. Anguished families were darting around in circles, carrying children, blankets, and anything they could immediately lay their hands on.

Although Iwan and Stefan had been working on digging the bunker for a considerable amount of time now, it still wasn't big enough to hold the whole family. They dug as often as possible, but it was time consuming work and, at this point, it was maybe eight-feet deep with just enough room for a ladder and one or two people to huddle in. For this reason, it wasn't the best option for Petro, Iwan, Daria, and their growing family.

Stefan stood next to the bunker and from across the way he could see Iwan by the barn. He watched as his brother released the cow, sparing her from incineration if the barn caught fire. He scanned the horizon and saw Daria with the boys heading for the farm wagon. He could hear bits and pieces of Iwan's voice screaming in terror over the sound of the gunfire. The bursts were getting louder and the soldiers were advancing. Surveying the scene was tortuous and Stefan felt helpless in the midst of such chaos.

"Daria, quick! Take Lyiubchyk and Lesio and get in the wagon," Iwan shouted.

"Iwan, I still have bread in the oven. I need to go back in," Daria wailed, knowing as she spoke that she was being irrational.

From the side, Petro grabbed Daria. "Daria, there's no time. Do as Iwan says. Take the boys and get in the wagon. We will meet you there."

"But what about Father?" Daria gasped.

"He'll be fine," Iwan interjected. "He's going to go in the bunker. That's why we built it. We knew this day was coming. Just go, Daria! Just go!" He tried to convey the gravity of the situation without scaring Daria and the boys more than necessary. But Daria saw a panic in Iwan's eyes that she had never seen before and so she felt a pang of fright she had never felt before.

Daria took one last glance in her father's direction—the old man locked eyes with his daughter. He gave her a strong nod and Daria knew this meant she must do as Iwan and Petro instructed. Anguished, she took the boys and a blanket and climbed into the wagon.

As she sat there, Daria watched Petro help her father into the bunker. She couldn't help but feel a slight comfort when she noticed that, even with the turmoil that surrounded him, Petro gingerly bent down to kiss the top of Stefan's head right before he wiggled the chestnut stump back over the top of the hole. Iwan, having let the rest of the livestock out of the barn, ran over to the stump and bent down to it. Both Iwan and Petro quickly but purposefully carved out the vent holes in the dirt that would allow Stefan to breathe. Just before they turned to leave him, Iwan ran back, knelt down, and whispered something to his surrogate father.

With an abrupt and purposeful turn, both Iwan and Petro sprinted back towards the wagon. By this time Daria was frantic with fear and both Lyiubchyk and Lesio were crying hysterically.

"Petro, just get in the wagon!" Iwan commanded. "I'll get the horse hitched up. Be ready to go. I'll jump in as soon as possible and we'll get this wagon moving as fast as we can!" The sounds of rifle blasts were quickly advancing—gun smoke and dust hung thickly in the air. Neither Iwan nor Petro could see much beyond a few feet in front of them—they held their gauze shirts over their mouths and noses as they made their way towards the wagon.

Petro leapt up into the wagon as Iwan quickly got the horse hitched up. Enrobed in chaos and fear, the horse instantly broke into a panicked lurch and the wagon pitched forward. Iwan jumped in and grabbed the reins. With life so out of control something so small as feeling the cold, smooth leather reins in his hands seemed to provide a fleeting moment's comfort. Iwan and Petro didn't know what they were headed away from, or towards, but they knew that having their family burned alive in their own home wasn't an option.

•

When they felt they were a safe distance from the path of destruction, the five exiles sat in the distant woods and waited. From the direction of their village they could hear cannons firing and rounds of ammunition being exchanged between the two armies. Plumes of smoke rose up and they could hear the bellowing of livestock burning alive. All they could do was sit and wait. No words were spoken, just looks of anguish and despair exchanged. As they watched through the trees, they didn't fear for their lives. They knew this military mission was not a mission of death, but rather a mission of destruction. But still they feared for their dear Stefan.

By late evening silence had befallen the village. Daria was grief-stricken with the uncertainty of her father's fate and was very anxious to return. While Stefan's status lay heavily upon her mind, both she and Petro sat obediently until Iwan gave his command.

●

After the minutes had quickly turned to hours, and with a quick tap of the horse, the wagon made it's descent back down to the little village of Krywen'ke, or rather, where Krywen'ke once stood. All that was left now was smoke, ashes, and the debris of weaponry. The horse had barely come to a stop by the bunker when Iwan, Petro, and Daria all bounded off the wagon and frantically began shoveling out the dirt around the stump. It was hard to tell if the ventilation holes had been deliberately crushed by the soldiers or just trampled shut, but the three of them feverishly dug, all unsure of the condition in which Stefan would be found.

Once again, Iwan and Petro had worn their fingertips down to blistering flesh. Finally, enough dirt had been removed to allow them to pry the stump from the hole. There they found Stefan. He was alive!

"Father! Father! I was so worried about you!" Daria sank to her knees and extended her hand to help pull him up. As she stared down into the hole, she noticed her father's face was an ashen white. He wasn't talking and seemed almost paralyzed with fear. His knuckles were as ghostly white as he was, still clutching to the ladder, gasping for air. The white of his exposed eye looked to be a cloudy mist and his stare was fixed upon his daughter's eyes.

"Daria, step aside," Petro interjected, gently nudging her away from the bunker.

"Stefan? Stefan? Are you okay? Stefan?!" Petro pleaded, smacking Stefan's cheeks to shock him back into the moment.

Iwan knelt down, too, and began gently rubbing Stefan's face and brow, trying to coax some color back into them. "Stefan?" Iwan tried to maintain a calm demeanor but panic crept in. Iwan softly peeled Stefan's fingers from the ladder and he and Petro lifted him out of the bunker. They laid him down on the cool dirt, smoldering fires burning all around them.

Finally, after what seemed like an eternity, Stefan took a deep breath and then softly spoke. "I'm okay, my sons. I'm okay." But, scanning his surroundings, despair sank in and he broke down. "Dear God, what has happened?"

All four looked in the direction of their home, but all they could see was smoke and flames. Each of them was thinking the exact same thought that Stefan had just voiced.

CHAPTER 6

Out of the Ashes

The house was made of clay with a thatched roof…the thatched roof had collapsed during the fire but the clay walls remained standing. The front addition was totally destroyed with only the stone basement remaining. Life changing decisions needed to be made by all—remain and rebuild or leave in search of an unknown future. For Iwan and Petro there was no option. They still faced certain death at the hands of the communists if they remained. Rebuilding would have to be done by others.

A HEAVY FOG lay thick over the smoldering village. The same scene played out everywhere as the villagers climbed out of their bunkers or ran back from their woodland hideouts only to find the fires still raging and the smoke enveloping what used to be their peaceful little hamlet. The hideous, rotten, burning smell was everywhere and they quickly recognized it for what it was—the scent of war and loss.

A circle of displaced souls emerged around the ghostly village. A circle of tired, red, troubled eyes waited and watched as a collective anxiety befell them. The lucky ones rested in their horse-drawn wagons, hunkered down together and wrapped in blankets. The ones who didn't grab anything felt little consolation other than having the clothes on their backs.

Wheels were halted and lives were thrown into suspended states of being. Confusion abounded...which direction would they head? If the horses carried them back to the village they would be returning to a place where there was little to nothing left. But now, even as the stars shone brightly in the early spring sky, the fear of what they would find in the other direction churned their stomachs. The unknown reeked of darkness and froze them in their tracks.

Stefan looked ashen and stone-faced as he sat in the back of the covered wagon. If the eyes are the windows to the soul, then Stefan's old soul appeared to be troubled beyond its years. He let his heavy lids close and immediately saw the face of his dear Maria. He could hear the footsteps of his children running through the fields around the house. He could see his neighbors who had lined up outside his front door to comfort him after Maria's passing. Stefan knew that a flight into the unknown was not an option for him. He had trudged and worked these fields so long that its rich, fertile soil was coursing through his veins. He had already cheated death once or twice—he had an eye patch and a piece of his skull missing to prove it. He knew that if death finally caught up to him it would be here, on his terms.

•

Throughout Iwan and Petro's lives, there had been many unspeakable moments. But what was becoming the peculiar norm were the unspoken decisions that had to be made and how, out of necessity, they were executed not through words but through the silent soul searching abilities of each other's eyes.

Iwan was lying down beside Daria and the boys under one of the only blankets they had grabbed. Petro and Stefan sat across from them bundled up in a few yards of cloth that were hastily thrown in the back of the wagon. Lyiubchyk and Lesio had that youthful gift of being able to sleep anywhere through anything and were fast asleep at Iwan's feet.

As the cold March breezes lapped at the fires and kicked up embers, Iwan glanced up at Petro and saw his brother's piercing eyes half looking for answers from him. It was clear that Petro was trying to meld his own logic with his prediction of his brother's thoughts, although he ultimately knew what the next step had to be. Silently, and without the utterance of a solitary word, the brothers were both resigned to the fact that, yet again, their lives were not their own. There were no real choices to be made, just ambiguous paths that needed to be followed. The communists would be back. If the two brothers fled alone, they risked saving their own lives at the expense of communist retaliation against their family through forced labor or, more likely, assassination.

This night felt ominously like the night before they left Mama and Father so many years ago. They were exposed and raw underneath the stars, with the trees standing judgment over the calamity at the heart of human nature. The brothers were frozen in turmoil, for they both believed that the path that life had chosen for them would consist of little more than gut-trusting navigation and more heartbreak from what, and who, would be left behind.

This time their angst was tenfold, knowing that one wrong decision would not only mean the end of their young lives, but also the end of Lesio's, Lyiubchyk's, and Daria's. They stoically sat through the gravity of the looming dawn and the renewal of the life-sucking task of staying one step ahead of the executioner.

As the first light began to reflect off the lightly frosted fields, and wagon wheels and horses began their tumultuous retreat, the small family said goodbye to their resident patriarch, Stefan, or now, as the children called him, *Didus*, or Grandfather.

Grief-stricken, Daria wailed, "Papa! Please come with us. You can't stay here. There's nothing left for you but ashes. Mama wouldn't want you to stay."

"No *malen'ka*, my *malen'ka Darusiu*. You know I can't do that. Mama is here. With me. I'm not alone." As Stefan cast a deliberate gaze over his shoulder the low-lying smoke still encompassed the remains of their clay and thatch house—a shard of curtain blew in the bone-chilling breeze. "I can't leave what is left. Apart from you, it's all I've got now. I would slow down your retreat and, would you just look at that wagon! There's hardly room for the five of you as it is. One more mouth to feed and one more body to hide isn't in the best interest of keeping my family alive…which is my only dream."

Stefan held his brittle hands to his heart and with a nod towards Petro and Iwan he continued, "The boys will keep you as safe as they possibly can. You will be better off with them than here with me. I wish more than anything in this world that we could still be together but time and fate has forced this division. *Darusiu*, I have raised you to be strong. I don't fear for one second that you can't help play a vital role in keeping your family alive. My only regret is that you are little more than a pawn in the game of wickedness that has pervaded this world. I will pray for you every day and will wait for the day you will *all* return. When that day comes I will be here waiting for you. I wish I had something to give to you, something to remember me by, should we never meet again. But they've destroyed it all."

Pulling his daughter close, Stefan whispered, "You have my heart. Just as you've always had it. It beats for you and will continue to beat for you until the blood no longer courses through my veins. *I love you, Darusiu.* Godspeed and know that I am always with you. Go out into the world and be a good person. That's all I ask of you."

"Oh, Papa!" Tears were streaming down Daria's face and her arms were trembling uncontrollably. Grasping her father tightly, she wrapped her arms around his neck and didn't want to let go. She soaked in every last moment and, breathing hard, tried to grasp and capture the smell of her papa, now masked with the charring of the embers that had dusted his hair. They both knew that the odds of ever seeing each other again were slim, but after losing Maria they had both learned one of life's cruelest lessons…how to let go. They had seen death in many forms and had already learned what the naïve would all learn one day: You can't take anything for granted. You can run, but your life is a script whose ending has been written by someone else. To fear death is to be shackled. To court death—even in its many forms—is to live.

"Papa, I will think of you every day and pray for your life and the life of our village. Please be safe. I'm begging you to find safety amongst the friends that are still here. And I promise that for you and for my family I will be strong. And we *will* be back. As soon as it is safe we will come back for you."

Iwan moved in to gently nudge Daria away. He clutched one arm around Daria and with the other he squeezed Stefan around the neck. Then, turning slightly, he gently kissed his father-in-law on the forehead. Then, pushing back the lump in his throat, he whispered, "Thank you. I give you my word that I will do my best to protect your daughter and your grandchildren. I *vow* to you that I will meet my own death before I will ever let anything happen to them. You take care of yourself and know that we are out here, with you, under these same stars. We love you, *Tatu*."

Petro turned to help Daria up into the wagon. With a final look back at her father, Daria's mouth shaped the words *I love you*. Petro took his seat in the front next to Iwan and as the wagon crept forward to begin its retreat, Daria looked down at the tears falling into her lap. Not betraying her promise to find the strength within herself, she didn't look back. Even though both had learned to *let go* through the loss of their beloved mother and wife, Maria, neither had learned...nor were ready...to say goodbye to each other. And both father and daughter realized this now.

Stefan stood in the middle of the main village road, one hand raised in a slight wave. As he turned to walk back towards the embers and smoke, he pulled a handkerchief out of his pocket and wiped his troubled brow. He watched until he couldn't even see the fog of dust from the wagon wheels, and then turned abruptly to walk towards what remained.

Very few other villagers had stayed. But, however down-trodden they may have been, the ones that did stay all found themselves filing back into the motion of life. Stefan bent down slowly to pick up a broken piece of his gate then ambled through what used to be his front yard.

Iwan, Petro, Daria, Lesio, and Lyiubchyk headed towards the Western Front in a slow procession of bloodshot eyes and heavy hearts. Fortunately, they didn't know then that they would never see Stefan again. The gift of ignorance was on their side and the opportunity of a new future provided the strength they needed to keep the wagon wheels turning.

CHAPTER 7

Caught in the Vise

A refugees means of transportation.
Photo courtesy of the Zapar family.

*We were in a caravan of wagons with thousands of displaced persons
who, likewise, were escaping to the West—away from communism.
Families who, like us, were caught in a vise between Communism and
Nazism, both of which squeezed the lifeblood out of innocent people.
Now we were literally in such a vise. Since we were traveling behind the
retreating German army, we could hear occasional distant explosions.
Some were cannon fire; others were detonations of bridges and other
military hardware. The Germans wanted to slow the pursuing Soviet
Communist Army.*

THE FIRST FEW days were bitter cold with snowfall measuring nearly a meter. Iwan and Petro had stopped briefly to check on Sergiy. His village had met a similar fate—though, fortunately, not nearly as bad, and he and some of his neighbors charitably offered the family some heavy blankets and enough linen to fashion a cover for their wagon.

Upon entering the Carpathian Mountains they cut down some saplings, bent them into arcs, and used some water soaked vines to hold the linen in place. They were now somewhat protected from the impending winter snows and piercing winds. Daria, Lesio, and Lyiubchyk stayed huddled under the cover but the wagon seat, manned at all times by Petro and Iwan, was completely exposed to the elements.

The German army was in hasty retreat and couldn't be bothered by slow moving caravans of horses, wagons, and displaced persons. More often than they could count, Iwan and Petro would watch in horror as a German vehicle would nudge a wagon, horse, and family off the road, many times rolling them into a ditch or, worse, a ravine...rendering that family's escape vehicle a crumbled pile of irreparable pieces. With just the clothes on their backs and whatever else they could carry, these families would be forced to continue their journey on foot.

About four days into their travels Iwan was at the reigns and the sun was high in the sky, burning a layer off the snow-capped foothills. Fortunately, this helped expedite their travel. But it didn't facilitate their finding food and shelter. Around midday, as they hit their stride, having logged several kilometers already since dawn, they turned a corner and came upon another family such as theirs with misfortune written across each of their faces. Quickly, they pulled the horse to a stop to see if they could offer any assistance to this family in need. Their wagon was completely overturned and destroyed but, fortunately, no one had been badly hurt.

"Brother, are you okay?" Iwan asked, staring into the pleading eyes of the stunned man. With angst on their faces, both the man and his wife looked up at Iwan and Petro.

Iwan moved towards the wagon and, steadying himself on the ground, grasped a plank from one of the wooden sides. "Maybe we can roll it back over? Let's try."

"Anything is worth a try," the man replied with a diffident tone suffusing his already shaken voice.

Iwan, Petro, and the man all climbed down into the shoulder of the trail and on a three count heaved the wagon over. It took a couple of tries to get it back on its wheels. Unfortunately, the wagon didn't stop when it reached its upright position—it continued to roll onto its other side, its splintered frame giving way completely.

With deflated spirits, the man and his wife exchanged glances. Then, with his eyes downcast, the man said to Iwan, "Please, take the horse. It's apparent that we have no use for it now. If it helps to expedite your safety it is all we can hope for. We will continue on foot."

Petro instinctively reached into his pocket in search of an offering for the family but instantly remembered he had nothing. Daria looked around their wagon for something to offer the children of the other family but, like Petro, knew they had nothing to give. As much as they wanted to be able to fix this family's predicament, they couldn't. By this time they were all far from home and knew they had to be somewhat selfish in order to preserve even their remote chance of survival.

In the same vein, this family quickly turned to the task of packing their slim amount of belongings into sacks fashioned out of their own linens so that they could carry their remaining supplies with them. It was every family for itself and neither side had hard feelings for going through the necessary business of their current situation.

Soon the second horse was hitched to the Zapar wagon and the other family had their belongings strapped to their backs. For a brief moment, there was nothing but the sound of silence and the heavy impression of burden and dread. The two women exchanged a final glance…Daria knew there was no way she could ever repay this woman for accepting the worse of the two fates. But with her chin held high and a firm nod of acceptance, this mysterious woman turned and began her march into the gray foothills. Iwan and Petro gave a final firm handshake to the gentleman and reiterated how grateful they were to the family for their sacrifice. Petro took the reins and now, with gathering speed, they continued onward until they could barely see the other family trudging through the snow.

Taking advantage of the additional horse, they pushed ahead as the daylight waned in an effort to get more distance under their belts. The trees started to thin out and they could see before them that they were getting close to a wooden bridge. There was a line of wagons crossing the bridge and soon it was their turn. As they began the crossing, their newly acquired horse seemed to hesitate. Shuffling on its feet for a brief moment, it paused, then quickly fell back to its previous rhythmic pace. After a few more moments, Iwan, Petro, Daria, and the boys were safely delivered to the other side.

Not a split second later, a thunderous explosion split the sky over their shoulders and plumes of smoke filled the air. Iwan and Petro instinctively ducked and Daria huddled the boys close to her bosom. The horses jumped in terror and began a fast gallop away from the ensuing flames. Looking behind them, Iwan and Petro could see that the bridge had been blown up and that those who had been crossing at the time had plummeted to their deaths. And there it was—that old familiar sound again. The sound of chaos, death, and despair. Arriving at a place a safe distance from the commotion, Iwan and Petro swiftly pulled the horses to a stop.

With a quick glance to where they bridge had stood just moments before, they jumped from the front seat down to the frosty ground and went around to the back of the wagon to check on Daria and the boys.

Daria's face was ashen. "I don't even want to know what happened. I can smell it, Iwan. I smell it! What did we do to deserve to get in the middle of all of this?" Daria pleaded. "How is this our life now? Dammit! Why do we deserve to live when all those behind us just died," she cried. "I'm done! I can't take this anymore. This is no life for us and it certainly isn't any kind of a life for Lyiubchyk and Lesio. If this is life I think I can handle death. I just want to pull over and stop. Can we just please stop? And hide. And wait?"

"Daria, I promise you, I will do my best not to let anything happen to you or Lyiubchyk or Lesio. And Petro, too. I made that promise to him a long time ago. We will get through this. Hiding is not the answer. Do you know how many ghosts are made from those who have chosen to hide? We need to keep this wagon moving forward in honor of those who no longer can. Death will catch up with us all one day but I'll be damned if I'm going to sit and wait for it to find us. We've run from it before and I'm pretty sure I've got it in me to run from it again. Do you, Daria? Because I need you with me this time. Without you and the boys there is no *me* anymore. You've got to be strong," Iwan continued his decree. "Remember what your father told you. You are the strongest woman I know and you've got to be even stronger now, for the boys' sake."

Petro joined in, "Daria, I love you like my own sister. And Iwan is right. We will get through this. We've all seen death and we've all seen worse than what just happened. I used to want to hide, too. This feeling you have is natural. It's just because running and escape is new to you. But we can't be sitting ducks. There is no surer suicide than that."

Deflated, Daria exhaled and then spoke with increasing certainty, "Okay. But we've got to switch. I can't sit in the back not seeing what's ahead. Let me sit on the bench for the rest of the way tonight at least. Petro, please let me switch with you."

Reluctantly, Petro handed over the reins. As he made his way to the back with the boys, he patted their new horse and then whispered in its ear, "Thank you, my friend. If it weren't for you we would have been on that bridge when it collapsed. I owe you one." He glanced up at Iwan, knowing he had heard and had thought the very same thing that Petro had just verbalized to the horses. Then, with one final look back in the direction of where the bridge once stood and perhaps in homage to the guardian angels that had given them the extra horse, he whispered a final, "*Diakuju.* Thank you." He gave a quick, firm nod in Daria's direction as if to say *Have at it* and then climbed the rest of the way into the back of the wagon and huddled up under the linen with Lyiubchyk and Lesio. While he would never admit it, he was glad for the reprieve and the solitude of his thoughts.

As Daria held the reins, she regained a bit of her confidence—and perhaps a little hatred for the enemy and a newfound courage to move forward. With a *Yah!* and tug on the reins, she again felt in control of the future...at least for the next few kilometers.

CHAPTER 8

Taking Chances

**The family's escape route as documented in
his handwritten account by Lubomyr Zapar.**
Photo courtesy of the Zapar family.

*Once the German army further retreated, we felt some relief and were
able to migrate westward at a more leisurely pace. We still needed to
flee with somewhat deliberate speed but had the luxury of catching our
breath from our recent brush with death. Since all borders into Poland,
Hungary, Slovakia, and Romania were guarded, many wagons with
families were being turned back—the border guards were not permitting
people to return home to their villages and to take their chances with
Soviet authorities. Because escapees were viewed as traitors by the
Soviets, Tato's (Iwan's) keen understanding of Soviet "compassion"
made it clear to him that such "compassion" really meant instant
death, or exile for all to Siberia. He decided that we would wait it out
in the Carpathian Mountains until circumstances changed.*

THIS PART OF the young family's life was known as the calm amongst the chaos. Although no one could ever really escape or even deny that they were in the middle of a full-blown war and were little more than refugees in a sea of the same, the caravans that had made it this far tended to stay together and the families found solace in the familiarity of things like recognizing a horse and wagon or sharing an evening with a person that looked oddly familiar.

Just like when their love had first blossomed several years ago within the tiny village of Krywen'ke, Iwan and Daria found themselves leaving Lesio and Liubcyhk with Petro and stealing a few quiet moments together—offering at least some ephemeral quality of married life to each other. While these moments were few and far between, they were never taken for granted. Deep inside they both knew that they were only one wrong turn or one mistaken gesture away from being torn from each other and having their new family be forever divided, if not annihilated. For this reason they would often lie under the stars and talk late into the night about all the things they were going to do if the world ever reclaimed its sanity and found a renewed interest in humanity.

On one such quiet evening, the two lay in the golden fields together, Daria with her head resting on Iwan's strong but hunger-withered chest. Iwan looked deep into Daria's eyes and softly spoke. "Daria, I need you to know that I've been thinking about us a lot lately as I hold those reins and drive the wagon forward day in and day out. And, while I know our love is true and pure, at the same time, I can't help but feel bittersweet about it."

"I don't understand what you're trying to tell me, Iwan," said Daria, softly. "I love you with every fiber of my being and can't even remember those days before you were a part of my life. It seems like a different lifetime altogether. But I fell in love with you for *all* that you are. You are so handsome and chiseled. I look at you and I see one of those statues from ancient Greece. All you need are some olive leaves around your head," she said with a smile. "So many times, even after a long day traveling from place to place I find myself exhausted but hypnotically staring at you, lost in my own thoughts of how beautiful you are—inside and out. It makes my heart flutter to realize that I have you. And it's not just your handsome good looks that made me fall for you. I love your intellect. I love your brain. I love how you think and I loved watching how you worked in my family's store and the way you made our business thrive. You are all that I've ever wanted. I am just glad you found me before someone else found you.

"And so now, for reasons both good and bad, here we are, under the early evening stars, and even though there is much danger both ahead and behind us, we are together. And that's all I've ever really wanted. I know each day may be our last but I can't think of another person I would rather spend my last day with than you...and the boys, of course." When Daria said *boys* she was also including Petro, as she often did. At this point in her life, Petro was as near and dear to her as her own brother.

"Here's the thing, Darusiu. I love you, too, more than anything in this world. I love the way you walk with your hands clasped behind your back...with more authority than any five-foot-tall woman should be able to convey," Iwan teased. "I love that you are such a wonderful mother to my two sons. I can hardly fathom how lucky I am to have you in my life. And most of all, I love knowing that even if, God forbid, something does happen to me, I couldn't have picked a stronger woman to keep this wagon moving forward and these children of ours safe. I love everything about you, Darusiu. Everything. It's just that I feel sad that you have taken on this burden of my life. You run because Petro and I made the choice to run before you were ever even in the picture...and that's beyond unfair. If I had never come into your life you would still be with your father in the relative safety of your village. Yet here you are...cold, scared, undernourished. Part of me feels selfish for having ever let you fall in love with me."

"I can't believe you would even say that, Iwan! With my whole heart I can promise you that there is no other path in life I would rather have chosen than the one that keeps me with you. Yes, I could be home in Krywen'ke trying to rebuild what was left of my village but even then I would still be running from something or someone. This world is not in balance. Evil is reigning and it's coming at us from every direction. No matter where I am, I am not safe. I would be no safer at home than I am right here with you. The way I see it, you had three paths you could have chosen. You could have joined the communists—that would have meant destroying lives. You could have been like some of our fellow Ukrainians and worked with the Nazi regime—that would have meant destroying even more lives. Both would be death sentences, and you'd be the one handing them out. You chose the third path, the hardest path, which is the path of goodness and humanity. That is why I love you and that is why I will be by your side forever."

With tears in his eyes Iwan said, "Oh, Darusiu. I love you!" He took firm hold of his wife, wrapped his arms around her, and gave her a tender kiss. Wiping some dirt off her cheek and whisking away a rogue strand of her reddish brown locks, he continued, "One day this will all be behind us and we will live on a little farm somewhere far away, where we'll never have to worry about shadows chasing us. But until then, you have my word that I will be right here. I'm never going to let anything happen to you, my dear, or to our family. Thank you for going down this path with me. I know it's not an easy path but I could never have lived with myself if I had chosen differently. And if I had, I wouldn't have been worthy of such a love as yours. Even in a world of discontent, you have made me a very happy man."

With no more words left to be spoken, the two fell naturally into each other, making love under the stars in the crisp breeze of the late autumn night. They were truly grateful to lose themselves in each other's physical beings, even if only for a few fleeting moments, before the dawn of another day of hardship and survival once again became the necessary focus.

●

During this time of relative calm, Iwan, Petro, and Daria did their best to provide stability for Lyiubchyk and Lesio. Considering all they had faced already, Iwan and Petro firmly believed that they could be stricken dead at any moment. And giving in to the bodily fatigue of everyday life as a refugee would mean leaving Daria and the children as sitting ducks. So each morning, Petro and Iwan would find food, water, and prospective shelter, and decide whether it was best to stay where they were or to continue on. By this point there was a news-filtering network that advised the refugees regarding their safety—road conditions, the state of border crossings, and the security of supply routes.

Although the brunt of the childcare duties fell to Daria, she wouldn't allow any form of reprieve from her fair share of the other daily responsibilities. She took it upon herself, in fact, to be ready should their momentarily stable climate rapidly deteriorate. Even at five feet tall she was able to swing an ax to help chop wood for the fires, and, though there was no actual place to call home, she busied herself with maintaining the covered wagon and helping with repairs when needed. When the winds weren't whipping she would take the boys out into the forest and teach them what vegetation was edible and what they should avoid. With Iwan's natural homeopathic and pharmaceutical background, she often had a wish list of items to forage for so that he could make elixirs or tinctures and store them in old bottles that they had found along the roadside.

Come nightfall, Daria was usually exhausted, freezing, or both. She would often collapse into the wagon when the time came for them all to pack in like sardines in an attempt to keep warm.

As the days passed, so did Daria's anxiety that she would be left to raise her young children alone. Mentally tortured but physically worn out, she slept at night. By day she worked and renewed her resolution that if she had to, she could do it alone. She knew she didn't ever want to, but reality forced her to stay one step ahead of death and complacency.

•

Daria, Iwan, Petro, Lesio, and Lyiubchyk had traveled as far as Yasinia, a town in the center of the Carpathian mountains, where they had endured a bitter winter finding food, making due with what shards of material they had to keep them warm, and watching some around them perish from poor health or lack of proper living conditions. Many nights, Iwan and Petro sat by the makeshift bedside of one of *the others* to help them greet death.

It was during these bedside vigils that the brothers found an odd peace. They would watch the physical world dissolve as the very soul of the dying person was freed. Both Petro and Iwan considered it a gift from the dying to the living—for what they saw they would never forget. With each and every last breath, the dying found peace. There would be no more cold, no more guns, no more running. Just a stillness. As the blood slowly stopped flowing so did the terror...at least for the dead. It wasn't a perfect scenario or pathway to peace for everyone, for the ones that were left behind became grief-stricken and were often inconsolable.

Some died with anxious looks of wonder on their faces, looks that made Iwan and Petro question what lay ahead. But some of the others had fought death so hard and for so long that even as death knocked for them they were fighting with every bit of their souls to stay on this side of the door. And a few, as they took their last dying breath, would have one tear stream out of the corner of one of their eyes as if drawing a final curtain on those they were leaving behind.

Before the war, if a loved one passed, there was the luxury of shutting out the world, at least for a few days, and allowing time for processing one's heartache. But in this new world, there was no time for grieving as the need to keep the rest of the family alive was greater than any personal need. The struggle had to continue unbroken, even through anguish.

To mark each death, Iwan and Petro would shut the eyes of the departed—perhaps to symbolize that the dead would no longer have to look upon such sadness. And then the brothers would say a prayer with the others. Afterwards, they would quietly and stoically walk back to their family. Why they viewed this ceremonious ritual as such a gift they found hard to wrap their heads around. The best they could figure was that they knew there was always a way out. Not that they wanted to choose death as their option but if, like the rest of their lives, this choice was made for them, they ultimately knew that one way or another, they would find peace.

●

After watching too many deaths and with illness running rampant in their camp, Iwan decided that a chancy crossing into Hungary would have to be attempted. Since hearing rumors about executions at the borders, others in the camp strongly advised Iwan to abort his plan, but Iwan adamantly felt it was best to try.

It was during this time that Nazi Germany and its allies were invading the Soviet Union and many Ukrainians and

Polish people began to regard these armies as *liberators* of their people. The policies of the Nazi army initially encouraged this hope of a 'Greater Ukraine'—a Ukraine finally liberated from the crushing hand of the Soviets, and offered these refugees an initial period of tolerance while feeding off the hopeful climate of the Ukrainian and Polish uprising. While neither Iwan nor Petro wholeheartedly believed that the Nazis offered them a true path to a new Ukraine, this path seemed less risky than capture by the Communists under their status as *traitors*. In the minds of these refugees, to move in the direction of the Nazi army and away from the Communists clearly seemed the lesser of the two evils.

So, at first light, Daria, Iwan, and Petro all hurried to ready the wagon for their travels. Daria skillfully folded the linen blankets and tucked them under the few pots, pans, and tin cans they used for cooking by the campfire. Not knowing how long the crossing would take, she had already gotten the boys up and cleaned their faces with some snow she had melted over the early morning fire.

The snow was falling heavily and Iwan and Petro had begun the never-ending task of digging out the wheels of the wagon from where it had been sitting. The makeshift roads were already beginning to get crowded. People were milling around and starting their day, so even through such a heavy snow, the treacherous roads were passable.

Upon their mother's instructions, the boys relieved them-selves one last time and then jumped back under the now tattered wagon cover, arguing over who would get the spot farthest away from the back, where the blowing snow was creeping in. Even in wartime, kids would be kids. As Iwan and Petro jumped to the reins, the horses gave a sighing heave and reluctantly set the splintered wooden wheels in motion, wheels which had been swollen with the dampness of the snow and were getting increasingly harder for the horses to pull.

Four other wagons were part of the caravan—one in front of them and three behind. The sun was getting higher in the sky but the snow and wind were not letting up. The brothers strained to see the wagon and the road ahead but the whiteout conditions were proving to be nearly impossible.

An unsettling feeling crept into both Iwan and Petro as they began to second-guess their decision. The caravan of five continued to move onward, though, and, being sandwiched in between the other carts, neither Iwan nor Petro felt they were in dire enough straits to cause them to stop.

So onward they continued—slowly, deliberately, and hyperfocused on getting this border crossing behind them.

Just as the snowfall began to wane slightly—as dusk was beginning to fall—a shadowy figure came into view. At first glance they thought it could be another refugee, like themselves, who needed their help. But as the shadow drew nearer they realized it was a Hungarian border patrolman. Eyes wide, Iwan and Petro shot a sideways glance at each other. Immediately their hearts began to race, knowing that their lives—and all the lives within their caravan—were yet again on the line and at the mercy of fate—or at least the whim of a stranger.

The man on the first wagon tried to pretend he hadn't seen the patrolman and tried to continue past. This irritated the guard who lurched forward on his horse and drew his 35M

Puska rifle. He commanded the arrest of the entire caravan as he drew his rifle to the lead wagoner's head.

Spitting on the ground alongside the wagon, the patrolman commanded the man to jump down off his wagon. The man instantly did what he was told and followed the guard to the next wagon, where Iwan and Petro sat with looks of stunned disbelief.

Over the years the brothers had learned that the less you say the better, so they made no motion and issued not a syllable. The patrolman nodded his head at the ground, with the rifle by his side—finger poised to pull the trigger at a second's notice. Taking their cue, Iwan and Petro carefully jumped down to the ground and stood there on the road. The patrolman knew he needn't fear their flight, because precious cargo was being transported inside each and every wagon—these men weren't going anywhere. So he continued his march up to each of the five wagons and pulled the men from their reins and their families.

Inside each wagon the same scene played out. The women hunched over their children, holding them in their arms. They shushed them as they strained to hear what was going on outside. Some of them, like Daria, peeked out through small tears in their makeshift covers and cringed at the sight of the rifle, and of the shiny black shoes that crunched through the snow towards them. Their hearts raced and they instantly longed to be back in the woods near the safety and sweet smell of their campfire. Collectively, they held their breath and waited.

Iwan came up to the back of the wagon, ashen, and matter-of-factly stated, "Darusiu, keep the boys close. You stay here. Do you hear me? Don't go anywhere. I'll be right back." Their eyes locked and he said it again, as if to add more certainty with the second pass, "I'll be right back."

Without a word, Daria peered out over the boys' heads. She quietly nodded as Iwan abruptly turned. She could hear his footsteps as they softly faded in the distance. Tears welled up in her eyes and she struggled to choke back the lump in her throat. The boys could feel her shaking and, despite their youth, they understood the severity of the situation they were now in. Not one word was uttered amongst the three left behind.

CHAPTER 9

Angels Among Demons

**Lesio (Left) and Lyiubchyk (Right) with
some of 'the others' along the way.**
Photo courtesy of the Zapar family.

The patrolman had asked each of the men to provide proof of authorization to cross the border and, since none could be provided, he escorted them all to a building that served as border patrol headquarters. The women and children remained in their wagons without any word of explanation. At this time during the war, any officer or guard was a law unto himself and could arbitrarily order freedom, imprisonment, or death at will, without any personal consequence.

IT WAS WHITE as far as the eye could see. The five wives and their children sat in the tattered covered wagons, held hostage by their own fear and silence. They had already waited nearly two hours—the snowdrifts rose to the top of the wagon wheels. The horses were restless, shifting from side to side in anxious anticipation of their continuing journey westward. But nothing moved. The air had that steely smell of snowfall and even through the bitter cold the wives felt nothing but crushing fear. Time stood still.

They could see dim candlelight coming from inside the cabin and a small plume of smoke rising from the chimney. The caravan sat idle in front of the makeshift border patrol about a quarter of a mile away—just far enough for the ladies to be able to remain fixated on the movements inside, yet too far to hear or see anything that was going on within the stone walls.

After one hour, they could take it no more. They decided to trudge through the drifts, children on their hips, and beg the guard to let their husbands go.

Cautiously, Daria opened the door to find her beloved husband, Iwan, and his brother, Petro, lined up against the back wall with three other husbands from their caravan. It was an ominous sight—perhaps the prelude to their execution. Daria couldn't help but remember Iwan's final plea before they had chosen this risky path for their young family: One way or another they would all die or survive together—but they would not give up. They would do everything in their power to claim this life that was theirs. *They belonged to no one.*

Falling to her knees she began her plea. "Please, I pray, officer, I beg you to let my Iwan go. You see he has a young family and without him we will all die in the snow. We are good, God-fearing people. Surely you have a wife and maybe some children yourself? You have a decision to make, I know. What would you do if this were your family? Please, I beg of you, spare these men. Spare us all!"

As she looked at the men lined up against the wall, a lump rose up in Daria's throat and she could continue no further. There was no chance to continue, however, as the border guard grabbed her elbow, whirled her around, and then began walking her to the door. Her two children clung to her skirt, fearing eye contact with the guard.

"You silly woman. Who are you to barge in here and try to tell me how to do my job? Who are you to throw my family in my face? They are of no concern to you and our people. We are not Ukrainians," he said with a snarl. "Your men have done something really stupid trying to cross and they must pay. They *will* pay. Out! Get out," his voice escalated, "before you and your children are made to pay, too!"

Daria collapsed and, not knowing what else to do, began kissing the man's boots. The other four women followed suit, wailing for compassion. The guard took his rifle and jammed it down at the floor, catching one of the ladies off guard and landing the rifle on her foot with a sharp thud. She wailed even louder and, at this, the men began shouting.

"Daria, leave! Get out of here. Everything will be okay one way or another, but get OUT!" Iwan forced a brave façade even though he could feel the cracks in his voice. One more time he yelled, "Leave! Get out!" and he saw his youngest son Lyiubchyk reach out his arm, as if to grab his *Tato*—his Dad, and bring him along. There was nothing he could do. He was helpless. His arm involuntarily began to reciprocate the gesture but he quickly dropped it and the guard slammed the door shut.

Just like that they were back out in the cold and the men were still behind the door. The ladies and children trudged back out to their wagons and continued their agonizing wait.

As soon as the door shut behind them, the border patrol took the men out the back door and lined them up against the house. One by one he pushed them down on their knees. They could feel each other's rapid fire breathing as each struggled to find his next breath. Iwan felt through the snow to find his brother's hand. He clasped it tightly. Neither one looked at the other but they could feel each other's pulses—they beat nearly in unison. Was this it? Had they come this far and escaped death so many times only to lose their lives on the whim of this guard?

One by one the shots rang out in their ears.

One. Click click.

Two. Click click.

Three. Click click.

From the wagons the ladies heard the same deafening sounds and their hearts froze. They couldn't move. They didn't want to face the inevitable so it was easiest for the women to sit and suspend the reality of what had just happened.

Daria put her head down, "Iwan," she muttered, "Petro."

●

The anguish these ladies felt was excruciating. Each one envisioned her world collapsing around her. Would they be next? What would happen to their children? Could they carry on without their husbands? Daria sat there, stunned. She hadn't moved from her spot in the wagon since they had been ejected from the headquarters. Lesio and Lyiubchyk weren't sure what had just happened but the sound of gunfire had been deafening and had startled them to tears. The heaving of their mother's breast only incited them to more panic.

"*Tato! Tato!* Mama, where's *Tato* and Uncle Petro? What just happened?" they wailed.

Tears streaming down her face, Daria said nothing. A chill crept into her body and this time it wasn't from the harsh elements she had braved for so long. She didn't notice the sun setting nor did she feel the tears of her children as they clung to her chest. She felt hatred. And loathing. And anger that quickly became trumped by her resolve. But she didn't feel scared or hopeless. And the absence of those emotions struck her as odd.

Daria gathered herself, covered the boys, and climbed out of the wagon. Just as she had done a few months before, she jumped up onto the front seat and grabbed the reins. She may have just lost her husband and her brother-in-law but she was going to make damn sure that she wouldn't lose her two boys.

She saw this brief moment as an opportunity. If the men had just been shot she was going to take advantage of the ensuing chaos. Death required cleaning up and she hoped that the guards were busy with that task. With the other ladies still clambering inside their wagons, she lurched hers forward.

Inside, she knew this didn't feel right but she figured it was her only chance.

From those many late nights talking under the stars she knew with utmost certainty that this was what Iwan would have wanted. She fought off the urge to run into the headquarters and grab their bodies as adrenaline and hatred coursed through her veins.

She tugged at the reins and her cart pulled out of the procession. The wheels moved ahead. The snow was beginning to wane and she gave one last look in the direction of the tiny little house that was the makeshift headquarters. "Iwan. Petro," she whispered. "I will do as you taught me. I will keep your sons and nephews alive." Choking back more words, she softly whispered, "I love you." Then she turned back to the road.

Not a moment later the guard ran out of the house with his rifle in his hand. "*Stij!* Stop!"

She turned to look. The patrolman was running after her. And behind him she saw all five of the men running in her direction, too.

She halted the wagon and was soon staring down the barrel of the rifle and into the eyes of the guard. Petro and Iwan leapt up to grab Daria as she crumbled in a heap of despair, wondering if she was going mad and these were really ghosts. Tears streamed down her cheeks, as she couldn't believe their fortune. Even the guard turned for a quick moment to let her collect herself.

Bowing to the guard, her gratefulness overflowed. "Thank you, oh thank you. I can't believe you spared my Iwan and Petro," she stammered.

"Please, you stupid woman," the guard stared her down. Then, with even more anger, shouted, "What are you thinking taking off like that? Get back in the wagon. NOW!"

"Daria, just get in the wagon. Please," Iwan said.

Daria turned and, before climbing back in to sit with her children, she gave the guard what can only be described as the start of a grateful smile and the shallow nod of her head. She didn't want to anger him more but knew she owed him their lives.

"*Diakuju*. Thank you," she whispered once inside the safe confines of the wagon. And, slowly, she could feel the bitter grasp of hatred slip away.

The border guard searched all the wagons to be certain there were no weapons and that the men were of no military threat. He then proceeded to let the wagons turn around and start back in the direction they'd come from. Their lives spared, these men knew this guard had granted them another chance at life, however uncertain it might be.

As they made their way back to the confines of the forest, neither Iwan nor Petro said a word. They thought back to all the things that had crossed their minds as they faced the ugliness of death. Petro had thought of his young nephews, and of his parents, of all the lives that he had seen so ruthlessly snuffed out. He now wondered how much longer he could go on like this and pondered whether death on this day would have proven a friendlier option than what might be waiting for them around the next corner. Like Daria, he too felt hatred and scorn, which turned to an ambiguous gratefulness as they were allowed their freedom. With so many emotions stewing in his head, he began to wonder if he was truly going mad.

In a parallel thought process, Iwan, too, was recollecting the impact of his brush with death. Like Petro, he had also thought he was ready to accept it. Of course, it saddened him to think of all the things he would miss about the boys growing up, but then he remembered that the odds of their getting out of this alive were slim to none, and that meant these boys may never have the gift of time in which to age. He thought of Daria with another man, but again, he had doubts that she would survive this physical and mental turmoil they were going through for much longer. He had seen too much and lost too many to really feel attached to this world, and letting go seemed a viable option.

But then he remembered back to that moment when his son, Lyiubchyk, reached out to grab his hand, and that snapped him back to reality. He knew he had to be strong and fight to keep this young family alive. He felt saddened and even ashamed that he could give up so easily. Inside he already felt dead—but he wasn't ready to give up.

A moment later he glanced back and thought of his beautiful wife, Daria, now sleeping in the back of the wagon with Lyiubchyk and Lesio. A small smile came across his face as he pictured in his head the scene he came upon as he ran out of the headquarters with the guard. With pride he laughed to himself and turned to Petro.

With the first sliver of amusement he had mustered in months he said, "Dammit Petro. I think she was really going to leave us."

"What? Oh, Daria?" Petro seemed taken off guard as he bounced back out of his own thoughts. "I don't understand. How can you laugh after what we just went through. Forgive me, brother, but I cannot find the humor in that right now."

"No, not humorous really," said Iwan. "But all those times you and I told her to keep those boys alive and leave us behind if she had to...well, I didn't really ever think she would do it. But damn. She sure would! I know it wasn't funny, but did you *see* her face? All I know is I don't want to see her pissed off like that again. But I'm damn sure glad she's the mother of those two boys. She'll make them tougher than you and I ever could."

Petro cracked a smile. And then they both chuckled. "You may be right about that. And she may have to do that again sooner or later because I'll be damned if I know how we got out of this one alive."

The brothers returned to their solitary thoughts, darting between life and death in their hearts. Tonight at least, they were going to continue to choose life. Not because it was an easy choice, but because they were still puppets in this war and that's what the guard had whimsically granted them.

Neither Iwan nor Petro ever spoke of what had happened inside the headquarters that day. And Daria never asked. All that mattered was that those gunshots were not for them and that they had *all* been spared.

That same night, somewhere in the woods of Hungary, that patrolman lay awake, eyes wide open, feeling that he had saved lives today, but also knowing that he had sent those men back into the fire. But at least his hands were clean. And the children still had their fathers.

CHAPTER 10

The War Still Raging

The trauma of this event left such an indelible effect on Mama that to this day she has an incomprehensible fear of snow. She must recollect and associate snow with a real threat to life. One would have to live through such a harrowing experience to fully understand the lifelong subconscious impact.

Our small wagon caravan turned around and made its retreat downhill. More rolling hills made traveling easier. Not daring to encounter a repeat]of our Hungarian border experience, Iwan prudently decided to wait it out until the war and political climate changed enough to allow the displaced to emigrate across the borders to the west.

TO SAY THE family was devastated to have had to turn their wagon around and head back to where they started would be a bit of an exaggeration. When flirting with the Grim Reaper, if he tells you to turn in any direction other than death you're more than happy to oblige.

As the horses circled back around, there was a certain comfort the family found in going into a forest whose trail they already knew. They felt instant relief as they entered their old familiar territory and became reacquainted with several other wagons, horses, and campsites—ones they had passed several hours earlier.

As the wagon wheels crunched through the snow, eventually returning the Zapars to their previous *neighborhood*, Iwan and Petro couldn't help but feel a strange sense of failure overtake them. Men and women looked up from their campfires and gave a slight nod as if to say, *Oh, you're back*. Still others looked at their wagon in disbelief that any wagon was coming back from the west at all. As far as these folks knew, either the borders were abandoned and easily crossed, or they were highly secure and everyone that had been heading east had been caught in the web as they were boldly pursuing their freedom. This was the first wagon anyone in these woods had seen returning from a border and Iwan and Petro may as well have had a trombone and drum set to announce their arrival back to their still vacant spot at the campsite.

Right on cue, the horses pulled to a stop and looked at their masters as if to say, *Now what?* Petro and Iwan hopped down and made quick work of digging out the snowfall that had accumulated in their spot during the day, making room for the wagon and for their family to rest.

Lyiubchyk and Lesio were already sleeping soundly as Petro, Daria, and Iwan took their spots huddled up in the wagon. The woods were now pitch black as the last of the campfires were snuffed out—the smell of cold mixed with moist wood filled the air. Even that comforting faint smell of the stifled campfires wasn't enough to make any of them feel warm and the three transients lay wide-awake looking into the darkness. They were enveloped by the complete silence that filled the air—but to them it seemed like stabbing noise. Judging from the moon, it was past midnight and none of the three could get to sleep with the reel of the day's events playing through their heads.

"Iwan? Petro?" Daria sought the comfort of hearing their voices before trying one more time to rest.

"We're right here, Daria," Iwan whispered.

Daria couldn't hold back. She unleashed the storm of emotions that had been brewing within her inner turmoil. "I can't believe how close that was today. I feel like I may as well be lying down with ghosts right now. I'm so relieved that you are here with me but I just can't help but think back to that moment when I thought you were dead. Not a day goes by that I don't think about the possibility of being alone. Not a day goes by that I don't think of you being dead, or me being dead, or God forbid our sons facing the rifle."

What started as a soft cry quickly grew to a sob. "Iwan. Petro. I understand why you did what you did so many years ago but this is *so hard*. It was easier to face the unknown before Lesio and Lyiubchyk came along but now all I can think about is protecting them and keeping them out of the hands of the enemy. It consumes me day and night.

"I don't feel like myself anymore. I don't know who I am. I used to think I had life figured out. But then I lost Mama. And that was quickly followed by having to leave Papa behind in a burned down house that we used to call home. Now what's home? This? This wagon? These woods? We're protected by nothing. And I can't help but think of what we have given our sons so far in their short lives. We have given them hardship. This is no life for them. This is no life for any of us. You know that when you feel bad for your horses, who are living pretty much the exact same existence as you are, that it is not living at all."

"Ahhhh, Daria," Petro broke in. "Believe me, I understand. I do. And you're right. This is no life befitting my two beautiful nephews or my lovely sister-in-law. I know it's easy to feel like you're not doing enough for your sons and it's not easy to fight for what you believe to be right. But you must realize that there is nothing more we can do but to survive day by day. You know as well as we do that these choices have never been ours alone to make."

Iwan quietly waited out Petro's speech, thankful for a reprieve from having to verbalize his ever-changing emotions regarding their situation.

Petro continued, "I used to lay awake under these stars and wonder. Wonder about Mama and Papa, wonder about some of my friends from the old village. I wondered if my friends were communists and I wondered if my parents were dead or near death in labor camps. On too many occasions I've watched in horror as life was stolen by the callous actions of some imbecile with a gun in his hand and ice in his veins. All I ever knew is that I didn't want to be a slave to a gun or to the imbecile behind the gun.

"But still I wondered. What would have happened if I had made this decision or that decision? Where would Iwan and I be if we had just gone when they asked us to go? And then I think about tomorrow and any tomorrows that might be ahead of us. How will I die? And if I do, will you and the boys be safe? How many more scrapes with death can we feasibly walk away from without a scratch on us?

"But, Daria, these voices in my head have been silenced, if ever so slightly. Maybe I'm getting numb to it but I've watched death and I'm not afraid. Does that make me want to jump out in front of the imbecile with the gun? *Hell no!* It makes me want to fight. I want to fight for a life for us all. A life where we can make our own decisions and these boys, my nephews, can run around in the safety of a home. A home! Can you imagine that? I want them to feel warmth...and love. I want them to take off in golden fields somewhere with nothing but a gentle breeze at their backs. I want them each to meet a beautiful and strong woman like you and feel what it's like to be in love. Hell, I still want that for myself! One day I want to make my own family just like you and Iwan have. And I believe...no I *feel* it in my heart, in its very core...that one day I'm going to do just that. Or, I may get shot tomorrow and that will end my dream," Petro snickered before continuing. "But here's the thing. We don't know what tomorrow will bring for any of us. We could all get snuffed out in the middle of our dreams tonight and never wake up tomorrow. Or, we can get up tomorrow and the next day and the next 10,000 days after that without incident. Do you understand what I'm saying to you, Daria?"

Shaking her head, with tears still streaming down her cheeks, Daria's breathing began to slow and she started to regain her composure. "Yes, Petro, I know what you are saying to me. But I can't help but think constantly about all the what-ifs in my life and, even though it's a little bit selfish, I often wonder why this all has happened to us."

"Ahh, but Daria. You are looking at the bad. Look at all the good that has happened to us! Lyiubchyk and Lesio, for instance. Iwan found you and I have gained a sister. And a formidable one at that! If life really had cheated us we would have all died a long time ago. But we didn't. Iwan and I somehow eluded the gunfire in that blood soaked river so many years ago and we all escaped the fires in the village. What I'm getting at is if you want to have any sanity left, which I know is an ambitious wish these days, you have to take things one day at a time. You can ask yourself what–ifs on a continual basis but that line of questioning will drive you mad. If I had known what we were going to face today I don't know if I could have handled it. That...that is the gift.

"So let's just shut our eyes and get up tomorrow morning and be thankful for another sunrise. Because, you know, it really is a miracle that, even through all the bloodshed and horror, God has created something so beautiful as a sunrise or a snow-capped mountain or the vibrant golden wheat fields during the harvest. That's what we need to show the boys. While this would never be the life I would choose for them, I know one day they will understand.

"Your sons' situation is better than some others who are also steeped in this hideous, horrific war—children whose fathers leave their breakfast tables to go off to fight for an unjust cause, children whose fathers find themselves being the imbeciles behind those guns we hear, behind the gun we faced today. Well, one day this war will be talked about and written about and the story I want the boys to read is ours—one of resistance...and of fighting for what is right. You are showing them the strength of a conscience and the humility of doing what is honorable. There is no glory otherwise. You are a beautiful example of fighting for your own way in this very perverse world. And I swear, Daria, seeing you behind the reins today as the wagon was leaving us behind made me so proud. I am thankful that my brother found you. I hope I find a woman as strong as you some day."

With a gentle smile, and squinting through the near pitch darkness, Daria kissed Petro on the forehead. "Thank you, Petro. I needed that. Right isn't easy and love is a hard thing to have to let go of. I thought I was losing you both today. I think we all got lucky. If we had to go back and do that again tomorrow I think we would all die. So, yes, you are right. I will try not to think about tomorrow and what it might bring but, rather, shut my eyes and for the last couple of minutes before I hopefully drift off to sleep I will be thankful to have you and Iwan beside me. I love you, Petro. Thank you for being a part of my family. I'm sorry I had to leave my father behind but I am so grateful to have you on this journey. But one thing I can tell you for certain..."

"What's that, Daria?" Petro asked. Even Iwan opened one eye and gently lifted his head to see what Daria was going to say.

"There is no way in hell I'm going back to try to cross that border again any time soon." Daria laughed gently yet there was a soft but uncertain tone in her voice.

And with that, they drifted off to sleep. And the wagon wheels beneath them didn't move for months.

CHAPTER 11

Shelter in the Storm

**Lesio (Left) and Daria holding Lyiubchyk while
biding time with their host family in Yablunytsia.**
Photo courtesy of the Zapar family.

*For three months—April, May, and June of 1944—we stayed
with a family in the village of Yablunytsia. Although this family
was in need themselves, they graciously shared what little they
had with us. Iwan and Petro helped in any way they could—pro-
viding physical labor and helping to prepare the spring garden for
themselves and other families in the village. "Will work for food"
is not a new concept.*

As other immigrants came through town, Iwan would ask about travel conditions and about the opportunities for safe passage west. He also inquired about conditions in the war-torn East. Hearing that the Eastern Front was heading in our direction, Iwan thought it prudent to move to a safer location. We migrated in a northwesterly direction to a town called Bolekhiv, where we stayed from the end of June through July with another equally charitable family.

Such humanitarian gestures by these fine people involved not only accelerating the depletion of their food pantries but possible political repercussions as well. Aiding escapees such as us was considered traitorous by the Soviets, with potentially dire consequences. Nevertheless, these families would not turn away others in need. They understood what the true meaning of hunger was and would graciously help those whose pangs were greater than their own. Such empathy was not only evident in the families that took us in, but in others as well. These kinds of compassionate deeds were repeated countless times and in countless places during the war years.

AFTER THE CLOSE call at the Hungarian border, days turned into weeks and months as Daria, Iwan, and Petro lived under the mounting pressure to provide as much stability and decent nourishment for Lyiubchyk and Lesio as was possible during the turmoil of the times and given their status as *traitors* to the communists. Every day was a struggle but still Lesio and Lyiubchyk thrived.

It was now late summer of 1944 and the oppressive heat had begun to fade and give way to cooler mornings and gentle forest breezes. The five refugees had found work and shelter with several different families for days or weeks at a time before moving on to the next village. Iwan was ever cautious not to stay too long in any one spot so as not to have Lesio or Lyiubchyk feel rooted in anything other than family. He also felt a constant debt to these families and so he worked hard and gave back in any way he could to compensate them for the heavy risks they charitably absorbed as they sheltered his young family.

Most mornings began with the first crowing rooster announcing it was time to start the day. Sunlight would begin to seep through the cracks of whatever barn had become their shelter for the night. It was rare for them to stay inside the confines of a warm house. Even when offered one, Iwan and Petro almost invariably turned it down. They felt so indebted by the humanitarian assistance being offered them that they were agonizingly vigilant about minimizing whatever risks they could to these families and their children.

●

The war had not stopped the boys from growing fast and for all intents and purposes, Lyiubchyk and Lesio were *normal* four- and six-year-old children. Just like Iwan and Petro in the times of *Talabarske*, the young boys had an exceptional closeness that only early struggles and precarious times could have molded. One was constantly looking over his shoulder to ensure the safety of the other and, just like in the case of Iwan and Petro, the younger of the two, Lyiubchyk, seemed to be the more cautious of the two, with a penchant for making prudent decisions.

Many a time Lesio would flippantly perch high on a rock over a stream, or climb a tree with treacherously thin limbs, only to fall flat out as his younger brother watched...and learned what not to do. Even at the age of four it was apparent to Daria and Iwan that Lyiubchyk was a leader. Oftentimes, when the boys were sent off by their father or uncle to help in the fields, Iwan would look to Lyiubchyk to police Lesio and ensure that he was staying on task and not trying to invent some frivolous contraption out of, say, a potato and a stick. But being just as enmeshed in the web of the world war as anyone else, the two boys grew up fast and seemed older than their age might have conveyed.

Needless to say, Christmas and birthdays were celebrated with love but not presents. From the generosity and hand-me-downs of others, the boys had accumulated a set of clothing that mostly fit them—jackets for when the weather turned, and each a pair of shoes that didn't give them too many blisters. In the warmth of the summer they nearly always went barefoot. This caused Daria a great deal of anguish as they often tried to enter their host family's house without remembering that the soles of their feet were dirty—a constant muddied brown, in fact. Even frequent romps in the streams never really got them back to looking as clean as Daria hoped they would.

Other than the clothes on their backs they had little to claim as their own. But since it was all either one of them knew, they didn't seem to mind much, and the lack of proper toys actually made the two become expert builders of *things*. In the afternoons when they had some free time, after they were absolved from helping the men, the boys would go to the edge of the forest and build forts. Even though they were just four and six, Lesio and Lyiubchyk had a knack for coming up with structurally sound forest shelters that would often grow to incorporate separate rooms and roofing to keep out sudden rainstorms. Sometimes, when they had lots of time on their hands, they would include a door strung from sticks and vines with a bunker to hide from the bad guys... because every kid back then needed a bunker to hide from the bad guys.

●

One day, much to their surprise, Lesio and Lyiubchyk came back to the barn and saw a huge smile on Uncle Petro's face. The boys had a look of astonishment because typically Petro had a furrowed brow and worried eyes. They were delighted to see him so happy.

"Uncle Petro!" cried Lesio. "Why the big smile? You look like you just got an extra piece of bread with your broth!"

Lyiubchyk set his sturdy little legs in motion and jumped into Petro's lap. Petro gave his little nephew a tight hug and said, "Boys! You're not going to believe what Uncle Petro has gotten for you. I hope your mother and father are not mad because it seems so frivolous, but I was able to work a barter for a little something for each of you."

"What is it, Uncle Petro?" they cried in unison, bursting with excitement and barely able to control themselves. In their young lives they had never gotten anything just for them that didn't serve as food or clothes and especially not *just because*. On one hand, they wanted to be excited that it was a gift of some sort, but on the other, they knew that the likelihood of it being an impractical gift for their pleasure alone was slim.

"You two never get anything fun to play with. I can see that you each have a real talent for creativity and I was able to barter a little bit of my time helping in a general store in town in exchange for these."

Petro reached behind the bale of hay he was sitting on and, still smiling from ear to ear, pulled out two pads of paper and two pencils. "I used to draw when I was little. Your father and I would go out into the fields around our home and draw all sorts of things that we would see. We drew houses, trees, horses. I wish I still had some of those drawings to remind me of home. My wish for you boys—for us all—is to one day have a home again. But for now that is just a dream. But that's even more reason for you to have a pencil and a pad of paper...for you to dream. Maybe if you sketch your dreams on to these pieces of paper they will one day become a reality. And, even though we are not in a place of stability, all of this will remain in your memories forever. Draw it. There is still much good that I see everywhere and drawing it will preserve it and make you even more appreciative of a day in the future when things may not be going exactly as planned. And even on those days, drawing things as you wish them to be gives you power over bad."

The boys were trying to be respectful and listen to Uncle Petro's sermon but they had already gotten their hands on the pencils. Lesio quickly began scribbling new plans for the forts they would build as well as documenting ones they had previously built, ones that they had really liked.

Petro had a continual smile on his face as he watched. His eyes darted over to Lyiubchyk, whose paper remained completely bare. Lyiubchyk had chosen a quiet corner of the barn and seated himself on a bale of hay, his back leaning against the rough plank wall. At first, he held the pencil like any four-year-old would, tightly grasped with every finger hugging it right about the middle. He got ready to touch lead tip to paper but drew back quickly. He reset his fingers a bit lower on the pencil, went to do the same thing and again drew them back.

Petro walked over to him. "Lyiubchyk? What's the matter?"

Lyiubchyk looked up with his big dark eyes. "Uncle Petro, can you show me how to hold this thing?"

"Sure." Petro motioned for his nephew to scoot over. "Do you mind?"

Lyiubchyk more than willingly slid to the side, Petro sat down, and Lyiubchyk perched himself on his uncle's lap.

Petro patiently guided the child's fingers around the pencil and showed him how to hold it. The two spent several minutes marking the air as Lyiubchyk had his first lesson in drawing—the fine art of holding a pencil.

"Now draw something, Lyiubchyk," Petro urged him.

Again, Lyiubchyk picked up the pencil and slowly placed the point down on the paper. This time he made contact. But right before he committed to drawing anything he lifted the pencil again.

"What is it now, son?"

"Uncle Petro, I don't have anything to draw right now. I don't want to waste the paper. I want to wait until I have something really important to draw."

Petro was nearly moved to tears. How, at the age of four, did Lyiubchyk understand that this tablet and pencil would not last forever and would not be easy to replace?

"Lyiubchyk, I understand. Go have yourself an adventure and come back with something really important to draw. Okay?"

"I will, Uncle." He carefully wrapped his pencil and tablet in his makeshift blanket of gauze fabric and headed back outside.

•

A few days passed in which Uncle Petro was so busy in the fields that he didn't notice that Lyiubchyk had been working on his best rendering of something he had seen, something he had deemed very important. When he was privy to see the drawing, Petro recognized it right away. It was the Nazi eagle, guns crossed, enrobed with a wreath.

"Lyiubchyk! What made you draw this?" Petro asked, trying to down play his surprise.

"I found this pin." Lyiubchyk reached into his pocket and pulled out what looked to be a pin from one of the German officers. "You told me to draw something important. I've seen these men. I remember these men. They have guns and shiny shoes and jackets. They must be really important. So I drew this pin I found because it reminded me of them."

"Oh, Lyiubchyk. That is quite a work of art." He truly was amazed at the artistry of his four-year-old nephew. "But, son, please know that guns and shiny shoes and nice jackets don't make someone important. Because, truth be told, do you know what I think? I think that *you* are just as important as them. *More* important. And one day you will do good things with your life. Do you understand what I'm saying? Being important doesn't make you a good person. And those particular men you saw are evil men."

"Yes, Uncle Petro." Lyiubchyk's voice cracked, feeling he had done something bad.

"I love your art and please don't think you've wasted this piece of paper. This is what you see. It is what you know. And for that I'm sad. But draw what you love and what you dream, okay? Because what's important is what's in here," Petro said, holding his hand over Lyiubchyk's heart. "And in here," he said, softly tapping his nephew's brow.

The next day, Lyiubchyk presented Uncle Petro with a drawing of their little wagon, parked in front of a barn, with five smiling faces lined up in front of it. It even had Mama with her hands clasped behind her back, as was her custom. Petro, astonished by how detailed it was, teared up slightly. All he could muster was, "This is beautiful."

●

Iwan and Daria's love was solid and continued to blossom even through the perils of the unknown that they faced on a daily basis. Daria had the typical motherhood struggles of too much to do and not enough time to do it. And that was compounded by the crushing anxiety she felt every time the boys ventured out of her sight. Her role as matriarch of the family was to mirror their host matriarch—whomever that was on any particular day—and to help with the household chores. She washed clothes, stored the harvest, and did her share of work in the fields.

Daria and Iwan still struggled to find time for each other, but once in a while they were afforded the opportunity to do as they did at the beginning of their courting—steal time down by some little creek that ran alongside one or another of the villages they were staying in.

Sometimes Daria would quietly watch Iwan's attention wander off to the rushing of the current, and she would wonder just what was going through his head. He would stand in silence, with worry on his brow, as his eyes—glazed and fixated—would seemingly scan the stream and sometimes the horizon for distant ghosts.

Sometimes Daria couldn't help but to run her eyes up and down Iwan's well-built body. He would strip down to his underwear and slowly immerse himself in the stream. It was almost ritualistic, the way he deliberately walked in, one foot at a time, always glancing over his shoulder at the riverbanks and the distant horizon. If he caught Daria looking at him he would quickly snap out of his thoughts and throw her a nod as if to say, *Hey, wanna join me?*

Daria rarely got into the water with her husband—she was content staying along the bank, dangling her feet in the current, as he splashed some water her way. She was so enamored by Iwan that she couldn't help but feel flushed and excited as she watched him. She still remembered him sitting across the table from her that first day they met. He looked almost exactly the same now—his youth had only slightly given way to maturity as he grew into his sturdy physique. She still loved how solid those arms of his were. Just as solid as that first time she squeezed them down by the riverbank.

Often she would lay her head on his strong chest, which she always loved to do. And she loved his firm, solid physique. Often, at moments like this when it was just the two of them, she couldn't help herself—she would grab him and pull him down toward her as he walked by. To her, he was perfect. Even during a war, the sexual spirit of humans cannot lie dormant.

One afternoon while biding their time in their latest village the two snuck down to a covert spot by the stream. It was a steamy day and Iwan wasn't taking no for an answer from Daria as he got in to swim. He lifted her off the bank and threw her over his shoulder and into the water. She was kicking and screaming. He knew she couldn't swim so he was careful not to take her out too far. But she always felt secure and trusted those arms of his and rarely resisted for long.

"Oh, Darushiu. I love you."

"I love you, too, Iwan. Is it wrong to be so completely in love and happy with you? I mean, given this crazy world we're in right now surrounding us?"

"Ha! Well, I'd like to think not," he said. "You're the best decision I ever made. Of course, you're really the only decision that wasn't already made for me by my mere existence in the world. *But* I like to think I make pretty good decisions when I have to," Iwan chuckled.

"Well, Iwan," Daria said, looking up into his piercingly dark eyes. "Please don't be angry, but it seems there has been another decision made for you by your extraordinary existence in this world. And I would say it was a good decision that was partly made by you, too."

"Oh, no, Daria. What is it?" he asked, not quite sure what to expect.

After a pause, Daria began, "Well, Iwan. We have been sneaking off down here quite a bit since we've gotten to this new village. And you know I have no self control when it comes to you, right?" she said, stroking his rippled chest. "I can't resist you for long."

"So you want me right now?" Iwan laughed hard. "Is that what you're saying, Daria? No problem!" He began pulling open her shirt.

"Well, that, too, Iwan," she laughed, grabbing Iwan's hands. "But let me start with this..."

Daria guided his hands to her now growing abdomen. She searched Iwan's eyes and said, "We're going to have another baby. Are you ready for one more?"

Iwan was burning with desire for his wife as he kissed her lips and then moved down to her swollen breasts through the water-soaked fabric that was clinging to them.

"Of course I am, Daria. And I can't think of one other person I would rather raise my *three* children with than you."

With that, he carried Daria out of the water and under the shade of a well-canopied tree and the two made love late into the glowing afternoon.

In the quiet moments afterwards, as the sun was setting, Daria blissfully forgot about the world around her and tightly pressed herself against her husband. But Iwan, although fulfilled and happy on one level, found himself drifting off to that ever-constant place of concern and anxiety. Because, truth be told, when it came to the thought of bringing yet another life into this craziness, he was utterly terrified.

CHAPTER 12

The River Crossing

In late August or early September of 1944 we departed from Turka, traveling in a southwesterly direction, over the crest of the Carpathian Mountains towards the Slovakian border, which was now open to escapees.

CONSTANTLY VIGILANT and ever paranoid since seeing their own picture in that village newspaper, Iwan and Petro had become experts at being attuned to the chatter of whatever village they found themselves in. Countless strangers who had become familiar faces to each other and thus confidants of sorts along the way had formed a pipeline of communication. A thin line of trust existed among them but a thin line was all they had. Most were fighting for their lives along a trail of chaos and were in similar situations to Iwan and Petro. They all lived in fear of being turned in as traitors and had to tread carefully.

Word had begun to filter through the makeshift camps about the borders being open and Iwan and Petro decided that it was time to make a move. In what had now become ritual, Daria packed up the wagon, aided by Lyiubchyk and Lesio, as Petro got the horses ready and Iwan gathered needed supplies to begin their voyage. They said their grateful goodbyes to

their host family in Turka and so began their second attempt
to cross the border.

•

The refugees were making good time for a few days but
growing winds and steady rain began to make their journey
not only sluggish, but increasingly treacherous.

While there were a number of decent trails to follow, these
trails were mostly out in the open. Many times they had to take
a more covert approach—bypassing villages and towns due to
the proximity of German troops in the area. This made for
some tough calls, calls that had to be made on an increasingly
frequent basis, due to swollen streams that seemed to cut
through their intended path at the most inopportune times.

"Iwan, stop. I'm not so sure we can make that stream up
ahead," Petro asserted on one such occasion. Petro would often
scan the area and make suggestions, but as usual he would
ultimately default to his brother's judgment call.

"I think we've got to go through now," Iwan grimaced.
"If we don't push through it's just going to get deeper by the
minute. But let me get out and check. Hold on." He jumped
down from the wagon and grabbed the stick he always kept
within reach.

He circled back around the wagon to tell Daria and the
boys what was going on and then he briefly inspected the
stream. He plunged the stick down to see if he could gauge
its depth and, in his mind, obtained enough information to
deem it passable. The water level seemed to be a bit shy of
halfway up the wagon wheels.

He nodded in Petro's direction and they began to cross. At the point of no return—a horse's length into the swollen stream—what Iwan quickly realized was that they had failed to factor in the silt bottom. The wheels became locked and the horses couldn't get their footing. Panic quickly set in.

The horses were unable to get any leverage and their efforts at forward movement were futile. They became alarmed and began thrashing about erratically with increasingly desperate motions. One of the horses finally lost footing and fell on its side, causing a pulling on the wagon tongue. This made it nearly impossible for the other horse, and the wagon for that matter, to stay upright.

Iwan and Petro were panic-stricken, stuck and sinking in a stream of silt and rushing water. The combined strength of the current and the tugging of the horses quickly transformed an already bad situation into a grave one.

It didn't take Daria long to realize the seriousness of the circumstances as she peered out of the wagon and, with that ever constant feeling of helplessness, held the boys tight to her bosom and began to pray. If the wagon went over, the odds of drowning were very high.

Knowing something must be done, Petro jumped down into the rushing stream and hastily untethered the fallen horse just before it took the upright horse down with it. Terrified, the freed horse instinctively swam to safety on the riverbank.

Iwan glanced up and noticed some movement through the trees. He saw a group of men coming their way. He quickly assessed that they were neither friend nor foe but rather some gypsies also trying to stay ahead of what would be their certain demise at the hands of the German army.

By the time the gypsies reached the riverbank, Petro was standing on the wagon's tongue trying to calm the remaining horse—he was having a hard enough time trying to remain calm himself. He saw the growing crowd of gypsies moving towards them with their own horses and cried out for help.

One of the gypsies tied a rope from his horse to the wagon and several other men lined up along the rope to help. With Iwan at the reins and Petro calming and guiding the horse through the water, the gypsy's mare gave an exhausted but heaving pull. With that, the wagon hesitantly glided across the stream to the safety of the other side.

After taking a moment to collect their nerves, and at the invitation of the gypsies, they parked their wagon at the gypsy camp.

The gypsies welcomed the strangers, sharing their food with them and giving them soft beds of straw to sleep and dry out on. While Iwan, Petro, and Daria were shaken from the crossing, the experience paled in comparison to some of the other events they had survived. They quickly put it behind them and decided to linger for a few days with their new hosts. They hoped the streams would recede during this time, facilitating a safer crossing.

•

The next morning, as Daria was doing the best she could to help out around the camp, considering her pregnant state, she was pulled aside by one of the older gypsy women.

"Ma'am, please, come here. I need to say something to you."

Daria looked behind her, thinking that the old woman must be speaking to someone else, but, not seeing anyone behind her, she crept closer to the woman. As she neared, she noticed that the woman was blind, yet she appeared to be looking right through her.

"Please do not be alarmed by my calling you over or at what I am about to say. It's just that, well, I am a fortuneteller of sorts, and, even though I am blind, I can see the lights of angels surrounding you. Do you know what I mean by that?"

"No, not really," Daria replied apprehensively, half thinking the old lady was off her rocker. "I am from a small village. We didn't have fortunetellers there. And I'm not sure what lights you see," she said as she instinctively looked up and around for any glowing orb that might be encircling her head.

"Oh, you can't see them, dear. But I can. You must trust me on this. Your angels called me to you to tell you that they are here and by your side. Do not be afraid of the road that lies ahead of you. The angels want you to know that everything will be okay. You will be okay and your family will be okay."

"Ha! Ma'am...wait, what is your name?" Daria started.

"Sabina."

"Yes, Sabina. While I find great comfort in your words, how am I to believe that you are blessed with this ability to see into my future?"

"It is okay to doubt my ability. For me, it is more of a curse than a blessing, I assure you. But certain angels draw me to certain people and it is with the utmost responsibility to humanity that I feel I need to get their attention and tell them what I am guided to say. So will you allow me this?"

"Yes," said Daria, but with a dubious look in her eyes.

"Madame, you have a heavy heart. You have lost both your mother and your sister and you have found yourself in this war surrounded by men, with no matriarch to guide you as to what or how you should be as a mother or wife. Is this correct?"

"Yes. How did you know about my mother and sister?"

"That is what they told me," Sabina said, looking towards the heavens. As I said, it's a curse of sorts to have to know these things. But they speak to me. They want you to know that you are doing just fine. They are proud. And they want you to know that perhaps you will have a little girl soon that will help fill a bit of that void." Sabina nodded towards Daria's growing waistline.

"Oh," said Daria, as she rubbed her belly and gave a soft smile. "Really?"

"Yes. Really. And for that you should be very happy. But they want me to tell you to be aware and to be careful. Even though you have made it through many rough patches already, as you have happened into this new land, there will still be many perils ahead. Stay strong for your family and know that you will make it. But also know that there is nothing left, no reason for you to go back. Do you want to tell me about that? That you have been thinking about going back? They are worried that you will try to go back to find your father. Know that he is okay but you must never return under this tyranny. You will put your entire family at risk if you do. There may be a time many years in the future when you can return but it must not be anytime soon. Do you understand that? Of your return, you must remember this...if you continue to love Ukraine or grow to dislike Ukraine, you will never be free. Only when you make a new life for yourself and your family, and find your own importance in a new land will you find the freedom to let Ukraine go. And when that day comes, you will be free from this hurt. I must go now but hold these words close to your heart and remember them as you go through the days ahead. Listen to me and you will live a very long life. Heed my warning. Go back to Ukraine, and you all will perish."

"Thank you, Sabina. I understand. I'm not sure how you know all that you know about me but I will take it as a sign and heed your instructions. Please be safe and I thank you for calling me over to you." Daria nodded politely as Sabina slowly turned and walked away.

Oddly enough, Daria didn't see Sabina again among the camp dwellers that greeted her the next few days.

•

After several more days with their gypsy hosts, the family decided it was time to move on. Every day and every turn of the spokes brought them that much closer to this new life they were making for themselves and an odd form of indifference to the world they had left behind—and, ultimately, their own freedom.

CHAPTER 13

Family Treasure

In addition to the events of the soon-to-be-finished global conflict, it seemed that each day brought us our own private war. And countless other families had their own similar perilous situations. During this time, we had to avoid larger cities, which were now targets of American bombardment. We were getting distressing news that the Soviet underground militia was attacking and shooting those fleeing to the West—they regarded these escapees as traitors. Hearing these reports, we made a nighttime getaway on a forest road to a village called Sepliakapati. There we encountered hundreds of refugees like us, all fearing for their lives.

We had reached the end of the road, as far as further escape possibilities by horse and wagon went. As the Germans were retreating, they were taking refugees' horses to help them in their own retreat, and, in return, were issuing redemption certificates for food in Germany. Astutely realizing these certificates to be worthless, Iwan clandestinely sold our horses to a shop owner in town in exchange for food and some other basic supplies and we continued our descent southwest to Uzhhorod, where we finally crossed the border into Slovakia.

SHORTLY AFTER LEAVING their gypsy lifesavers, the five did what had by now become commonplace...they set up a temporary camp so that they could bide their time as they decided what to do next.

After so many close calls trying to get out of Ukraine, one would think that Iwan, Daria, and Petro could have breathed a sigh of relief. But this was still not only a terrifying time, but a bittersweet one for them all. Just as Daria had been told by the fortuneteller, Iwan and Petro had known since that day thirteen years ago when they crept out of their childhood home at dusk that their number one goal must be to leave Ukraine and never return. They had tirelessly made decisions and followed the path laid out before them, the path that would ultimately lead this family past the border and into a new land—hopefully, a land of freedom and security but that path was still far from determined.

What none of the three had foreseen was that a feeling in their gut that they had been sucker punched would appear once they got to the other side. They loved Ukraine. It was their heritage, their culture, and their family. It was blue skies, rolling hills of gold, ambling streams, and lush forests. It was a land of beauty and it was hard to leave. And it was even harder knowing that they would never be able to safely return.

But there was no looking back now. Even though it had been over a decade since the communists had issued their conscription notices, they were still lurking in the shadows, waiting patiently with their rifles, itching to carry out death sentences on those who had fled all those years before. But *the others* were still out there, too. Just like Iwan and Petro, there were hundreds that had suffered the same sort of horrifying events that Iwan and Petro had, and they were still alive... still existing in their own shadows...trying to stay one step ahead of evil. Not only was there the continual necessity of steering clear of the Soviets, but friendly fire from the Allies was an additional threat and a constant and imminent danger.

As they took some time to strategize about their next move, Iwan and Petro began their usual bartering of labor for food and supplies. With the horses sold they now had something they hadn't had in years—money.

One day Petro saw Iwan toiling over a wooden trunk that they had found abandoned alongside the road. He couldn't understand what Iwan was doing so he walked over to investigate. He found Iwan routing out a groove in the walls of the trunk underneath where the ledge would have been to support the top bin.

"Iwan, what in the world are you doing?"

Iwan looked up from his work and nonchalantly said, "Playing the game, brother. Playing the game."

"What's that mean? Can I help you with something?"

As had become his habit, Iwan peered in all directions to make sure they were alone before he spoke. "Brother, you mustn't say anything but, as you know, we have a little bit of money now from the horses and a couple of other trades we made in the village over the past few days. I've heard from others that the Germans are taking all gold and valuables coming across their borders. Our few gold rubles are too precious for us to lose. Although it's not much, it's something. And it's more than we've had in years. If we make it to Germany this will help us catch our breath before we figure out where to live and what we will do for work."

"So what's your plan here, brother? I'm not seeing it," Petro said.

"Well, just watch. I'm nearly done. And I'm glad you're here. I wanted you and Daria to know about this anyway. Just in case." Iwan looked up briefly to ensure he had his brother's attention and then went back to work.

He returned to routing out a notch that was cut deep into the sides of the trunk but razor thin enough to hold the coins securely. He reached in his pocket and took out twelve gold rubles, which was all the money they had to their names. Carefully, he slid the rubles into the groove and when they were all resting safely within it, he took a borrowed hammer and re-tacked the wooden strip over the slit.

"Ingenious, Iwan. What would we do without your good sense?" Petro smiled.

"You'll thank me one day." Iwan winked.

CHAPTER 14

The Round Up

October 1944

Realizing the war was in its last desperate phase, Germany needed a labor force to keep its factories running in order to supply their soldiers on the front lines. The Germans considered all of the Displaced Persons (DPs, as they came to be known) as a readily available work force. This work force, along with their families, was therefore rounded up and placed into railway boxcars to be taken to Germany as slave laborers. After several days of rounding up the teeming escapees who were trying to outrun the pursuing Soviets, the train began its long trip to Germany.

THE SMELL OF dampening campfires infiltrated the makeshift commune in which the brothers now found themselves, somewhere along the Slovakian border. Darkness was settling on the camp. Mothers held their children tight and men stared up at the stars, looking for answers. Daria was drifting towards sleep—Lyiubchyk and Lesio were cradled, one under each arm, around her expanding waistline. Iwan and Petro had just lain down and covered up as best they could to insulate themselves from the crisp air of midautumn. Quiet soon enveloped the camp. So, too, did the usual fear of what may be lurking beyond this temporary encampment.

Just as Iwan was finally able to drift into a deep sleep something began to vibrate the earth underneath him, eventually awakening him and jolting him to a full upright and alert position. Instinctively, he looked around for Daria and the boys and saw them begin to stir, too. Then he looked over his shoulder for his brother and saw that he was doing the exact same thing. Petro's eyes were wide open as he and his brother both scanned the darkness trying to come to full consciousness as quickly as possible so they could begin to grasp what was going on.

"Do you hear that, Iwan?"

"Yes. I hear it."

"What do you think it is?"

"I don't know," Iwan responded, his body rigid, not even remotely budging.

The vibration of the earth was in full crescendo as Daria and the boys groggily began to sit up and make their own sleep-worn assessment of what was going on.

"Iwan? Petro? What's happening?"

Their hearts were pounding and quickly the entire camp, in unison, was thinking the exact same thing. What *was* happening?

Without time to think, everyone began to do what had become instinctual these days. They gathered what they could and ran for the woods. Running as quickly as possible away from the approaching noise, which, beyond a shadow of a doubt, could only be the sound of tanks, military vehicles, and war yet again.

Iwan grabbed Lyiubchyk and tugged Daria along by her hand—she had a death grip on both. Petro, who always had a naturally calming demeanor with the children, grabbed Lesio, squeezed him tight to his chest, and incited him not to cry. "It's going to be okay, my dear nephew. Everything will be okay. We are just going to go into the woods until all of this passes. Okay?"

Lesio was mildly consoled. He nodded but a look of terror filled his eyes and he held his breath. He was being shaken up and down as Petro darted into the woods. Petro, at all times, kept his eyes fixated not on what was going on around him, but rather on his brother. He couldn't risk separation from Iwan. Both brothers knew that their strength had always been, and would continue to be, dependent upon each other.

And just like their hurried escape so many years before, the footsteps of the others around them filled their ears as their brains tried to grasp what was going on and what to do next.

The terrain of the forest mixed with the fast-paced anxiety of their footsteps made for treacherous running conditions. Gnarled roots meant twisted ankles and the brothers heard many people hit these roots and fall flat on their faces. The lucky ones were able to get up and continue their run but the unlucky ones were stopped in their tracks by a sprained or, God forbid, broken ankle. The dampness of the evening dew combined with the fallen and decaying leaves made it even worse. The slipperiness, plus Daria's condition, precluded the family from running very far. Once they were hidden a safe distance into the woods, Iwan stopped in his tracks and pulled the rest of the family down behind a boulder. From there they could see the flashlights moving about their campsite and they could hear the movement of the telltale German boots and long trench coats swishing about.

"What now, brother?" Petro asked.

"I have no idea," Iwan responded. All eyes were fixed on the soldiers.

They had barely managed to put a kilometer between themselves and the campsite. Each breath they took seemingly lasted a minute as they desperately struggled to figure out what was going to happen next. What were the Germans looking for? What were they going to do?

One of the German guards stopped in his tracks and stared off into the woods. Then he yelled something in German that none of them understood. As best they could tell he sounded agitated and upon his call the other soldiers began to march into the woods. It seemed as if a few of the guards hung back at the camp while the majority rapidly sped their footsteps up and began to run right in the direction of where Daria, Iwan, Petro, and the boys were hiding.

"Shit," Iwan exclaimed. Rapidly, his brain kicked into overdrive as he tried to find an out. But there wasn't one. Like the roaches that they were, the German army dispersed at a feverish pace, and before they knew it, one of the guards was standing right behind them, his gun cocked, screaming something so harshly that spit was flying out with every harsh syllable his tongue produced.

Lesio and Lyiubchyk were terrified but fortunately the guard let them remain with their father, uncle, and mother. There was no need to know a word of German. It was obvious that they needn't make any more decisions. The rifle pointed in their direction was in control now and led them back towards their original campsite.

They weren't the only ones who hadn't escaped. Nearly all the refugees ended up right back where they began—they were huddled together in the center of the clearing, encircled by those German soldiers who had remained behind to manage them. Rifles were cocked and ready to shoot and there simply were no options other than to succumb to their control.

At this point Daria stood between Iwan and Petro—her children tightly gripped in each hand. She had tears streaming down her face but she dared not make a sound for risk of execution. She could feel her own heart racing and could hear her steadfast companions as they, too, were in a suspended state of terror. She could also feel the twisting and turning of her unborn baby from deep in her womb and was, for a brief moment, relieved that she had one less trembling hand to hold. Fortunately, her boys knew all too well to stand silent and not make a noise. They learned very early the unspoken wartime mantra for children: *Don't cry or they will give you something to cry about.* So, stoically, even at the ages of four and six, the boys stood, their young hearts pounding and their naïve brains not fully able to grasp what might be about to happen.

One soldier came over to Lyiubchyk. As the little boy looked up towards the soldier's face, his gaze fell upon something instantly recognizable. The pin. That very pin with the eagle and the rifles enrobed in the wreath that he had drawn not so long ago. He remembered when Uncle Petro said that having a rifle didn't make you important but now all of that seemed very much a lie. Even as the man gave Lyiubchyk a pitiful half smile, Lyiubchyk knew that this man was very important.

•

Deep into the night, the families stood in the clearing surrounded by the soldiers. They were eventually allowed to gather what they could from their sites and lay on the cold, hard, damp earth to rest. Daria was too tired and too pregnant to stay awake even under the duress of the turn of events or their spartan sleeping conditions.

Judging by talk among the others that were fleeing west, and as best Iwan, Petro, and Daria could deduce from the few people that knew a smattering of German, they were to be transported by train to serve some time in the German labor camps. For all they knew, this was a better option than sleeping on the ground and trying to stay ahead of the Communist Army. But still they found themselves entwined in the bitter grasp of this fascist army and, because of that, they were very apprehensive.

CHAPTER 15

Friend or Foe?

In late October 1944, numerous obstacles interrupted the train ride to Germany. The American Air Force was now heavily bombing factories, roads, bridges, and railroads in order to deter the German movement of troops and supplies. Whenever tracks were damaged, making them impassable, the train would be stopped until repairs were completed. Those on board would take advantage of these stops to prepare some quick meals or attend to other necessities, or just to breathe some fresh air. This was a welcome reprieve from the confines of the tightly packed boxcars. Petro or Iwan would always take turns staying in the boxcar to make sure our few staples were not stolen. Hunger has no honor, so survival by whatever means necessary, even theft, was the rule of the day.

THE TRAIN HAD been rolling for several days already—perhaps nearly a week by this point. It was becoming increasingly hard to keep track of the days, as every day was a near duplicate of the previous one. Hills and fields glided by the windows and the boxcars were packed and stagnant. But still there was a gift—these displaced Ukrainians were treated more compassionately than the inhabitants of the parallel universe running alongside theirs, the Jewish one. And the Zapars were fortunate because they were still together as a family. They still had their children by their side.

For the first time in a long while, Iwan actually had time to reflect. And since there wasn't much else to do, he found himself in a constant struggle between thinking and trying to quell his thoughts.

On one such day, Iwan was sitting up against a wall with his knees pressed to his chest. He was listening as Lesio, who was sitting in Petro's lap, was discussing with his uncle the different contraptions he wanted to make when the boys got back out to the fields.

As the discussion continued, Lyiubchyk, although still stingy with the use of his pad of paper and pencil, had finally given in to complete and utter boredom and found himself increasingly uninhibited with his drawing while on the train. He was sitting next to Iwan staring at the blank piece of paper in front of him, patiently waiting for his father to finish shaving his pencil into a perfect point, when he placed the pad down on his lap, cocked his head sideways at his father, and said, "Father, why is it that we've never seen a picture of your and Uncle Petro's mother and father. Do you not have one?"

Iwan began to think of just how pertinent that question was right now, as they sat on their very own train on their way to a labor camp just as he was told his parents had done years prior. Is this what his father and mother had been feeling? But they didn't even have their sons by their sides like Iwan did. What had happened to them?

In order to overcome their own guilt he and Petro had decided long ago that the best way to move forward was to block out all the what ifs. They were powerless pawns in this new world, after all, and even if they knew where their parents were they still would be helpless in getting them back.

But the subconscious is a powerful thing and even though they never allowed their thoughts to stray to the beginnings of their evasion of the communist system that night, Iwan found his mother and father creeping into his dreams. There weren't different dreams. There was just one. It was always the same and recurred frequently.

Iwan would drift off to sleep and find himself in this fog waking up to his mother and father right in front of him. "Mama! Father!" he would plead. "What are you doing? Where have you been? I've been looking all over for you. I thought you died. I thought for sure that they killed you but here you are. Why didn't you come find us? Where have you been? Please tell me where you are so I can come see you. Please?"

In the dream, just as in life, his questions always went unanswered. In Iwan's mind there were no answers and there never would be. All that was left was frustration and doubt.

As all of these thoughts swept through Iwan's mind in a quick reel, Lyiubchyk readied himself for his father's answer. Finally it came.

"Well, Lyiubchyk. That's a hard question to answer. Because, you see, I don't really know where my mother and father are. And I don't really know if they are alive or dead. I know that's probably not the answer you were looking for but that's the only answer I've got. I promised myself a long time ago that I would never fill your head with misinformation or needless hope. Don't get me wrong. I always want you to have hopes and dreams, but you must keep them grounded in reality. I hope and dream that I will see my mother and father again some day. But I can't promise myself that it will happen because, well...you see our predicament here, yes?

"But it's like this, Lyiubchyk. It's like this. What I see, when I think of Mama and Father, is our dinner table. I see them so clearly sitting around our dinner table and we are talking about nothing important. Just things like the weather and how the crops are coming along. It doesn't sound like much but it was normal. It was *our* normal...and, oh, to go back to those days of normal, huh?"

Lyiubchyk, thinking he understood what *normal* was, nodded emphatically.

Iwan continued, "This is what I think. I think that one day we may all meet again. It may be here or it may be in Heaven. But regardless, we will all be together eventually. And think about it like this, Lyiubchyk. Every day is that day. Every day is the day we strive to get back to when we are sitting around the dinner table talking about nothing important because it is the day we are together. And we have that right now, on this very day. You see, we are together and you and I are talking, father and son. Sometimes we are talking about really important stuff, like this, and sometimes we are talking about really boring stuff, like Uncle Petro's funny hair when he wakes up in the morning," he chuckled, "but one day we may not have this, and this moment is what we will desperately long to get back to. So that is what I am going to do—enjoy this moment. And that is exactly what I hope you will do for the rest of your life. Does that make sense?"

"Yes, Father. It does. Even though today is kind of boring, one day I'll miss it." And with that he flipped through his sketchbook and turned to the first page, to the picture he drew weeks before, the one of the family standing in front of that barn, all full of smiles next to the horses and the wagon. And he said, while rubbing his hands gently over the drawing, "One day I'll miss today in the same way that I miss this day with Uncle Petro."

"Yep. That's it. I think you're understanding, son."

Iwan patted Lyiubchyk's knee and pulled him in close. In his own silence he was struggling to find a hope as innocent as his son's. Hope that they had many more days together.

•

The passengers could feel the train grinding to a halt. The soldiers were all at full attention—rifles at the ready—to ensure that there were no thoughts of fleeing in the heads of any of the prisoners. Iwan, Petro, Daria, and the boys began what had become the ritual at stops such as this. Iwan and Petro took turns carrying their trunk out with them, and Daria prepared what little sustenance they still had stored in the trunk around a small fire. The boys tried to get out some pent up energy running the fields and collecting rocks, sticks, and whatever else they could find.

On this particular day, the train had stopped alongside a dry cornfield where the stalks were speckled with black and beginning their decomposition, in homage to the approaching winter. All of the passengers had dispersed as much as they possibly could under the watchful eyes of the guards—which wasn't much at all—when they began to hear a low rumble from the sky above. Then the earth below their feet began to tremble.

At first, they all stopped dead in their tracks, trying to figure out what was going on. A look of panic on the guards' faces quickly intensified their own fright and they all began to run away from the train as hurriedly as they could. Running alongside them were the guards, in very much the same manner. Tattered shoes and shiny boots ran side by side in a perverted unison.

They were running so fast the stalks of corn were whizzing by in their peripheral vision, even slapping them in their faces at times. Daria had rounded up the boys and was running as quickly as her pregnant body possibly could, gripping Lyiubchyk's and Lesio's hands so tightly that they were a tangled mass of white knuckles. Iwan and Petro ran side by side, each holding one handle of the family trunk.

As fast as their legs gained speed, the low rumble in the sky became a shrill and deafening shriek through the clouds. Even though the passengers were kept in the dark about where exactly they were being taken, they knew with complete certainty that these planes were there for no other reason than to bomb the train they had been on just moments earlier.

Further and further into the cornfield they fled. Iwan and Petro kept a close distance behind Daria and the boys so that no one would be split up. Their feet ached and their ears were splitting.

Iwan looked up—he could see a formation of fighter planes coming their way. The Allied force of American planes looked to be seeking vengeance on this German train. In an instant, the rapid bursts of gunfire were added to the already deafening chorus.

With those first cracks of gunfire ringing in his ears, Petro stopped in his tracks and screamed, "Quick. Hit the ground! Daria, Lesio, Lyiubchyk, hit the ground!"

He and Iwan slammed the trunk and their bodies down on the ground and into the hard earth. Then, they quickly pulled their chests up just high enough to be able to scan the field for the rest of their family.

They could hear the boys screaming and through the thickening smoke they could see Daria looking up at the sky, making her own assessment of what was going on. Quickly, she pulled the boys' hands down towards the ground and they all hit the cool, clay-like mud oozing between the stalks.

Thinking that she could shield the boys with her own body, she threw herself on top of them. Not knowing what to do at this point, both boys had their hands over their ears, fighting hard to muffle the terrible sounds ringing in the air.

All at once a horrible blast consumed the area right alongside the train tracks and a putrid, hot blast of air made it a struggle to breathe and to stay huddled on the mud. The entire earth recoiled under them as scorched pieces of the corn stalks began to fall from the sky. The popcorn sound of the gunfire continued in unison with the blast and no one dared make a move. Time stopped and took on a surreal, slow quality as their heartbeats pulsed and became nearly as deafening as the air strike.

However long the attack went on, it ended almost as quickly as it had started. The American pilots must have realized that this train was not transporting German soldiers but, rather, civilians, and quickly terminated the attack. And fortunately for them all, during this time, precision bombing was only relatively precise and the bomb fell a good distance from the train.

An eerie calm befell the train stop and slowly, they climbed out of the mud and back onto their feet. There was a paralyzing feeling of relief that overcame them as they watched each other stand up.

The five of them were still alive, and, other than yet another horrible memory emblazoned in their psyche forever, they were unscathed. They brushed as much mud as they could off of their clothes and patted their hair to get the confetti of ash out. Everyone was still very shaken up but slowly they began to amble around.

What they saw was horrific. Not everyone on that train had been so lucky. A good deal of the gunfire had hit the unintended targets, these civilians, as many bodies lay motionless amid the stalks.

The train was hardly damaged and the guards began to make emergency repairs to get it up and running again as quickly as possible. During this time they allowed the prisoners a few moments to mourn their dead and to cover them with a minimal layer of dirt and corn stalks. Other than that, the corpses were left to the elements.

Daria sat close by, soothing the boys, as Iwan and Petro went about the field trying to locate the dead and help with the *burials*. They said a prayer over the bodies—a prayer they had created, memorized and unfortunately had become quite accustomed to saying during their time as comforters and gravediggers.

"Oh Lord, please bless this man, and please expedite his soul to a more heavenly place than this. Please, may he have learned from

you his lesson here on Earth, so that upon his return to a new world of your choosing, he may again have the untethered ability to bring joy and happiness where darkness lay. Please guide those left behind down a path of righteousness, forgiveness, and ultimate freedom— freedom from this web in which we all are caught. And one day may you find the dark corner of this life where these evil shadows lurk, and may you hand out swift justice for their actions against mankind. Until we meet again, my friend, may peace and love guide you to your eternal home."

With hearts of lead, the brothers returned to the train where Daria, Lesio, and Lyiubchyk were already waiting. By their count just prior to stepping aboard, twenty-four souls had been lost that day. Twenty-four souls were dead and gone, their bodies left to rot in the elements.

Just before climbing back on to the train, Petro looked at his brother pensively. The only words that came to him were, "God save us, brother." He hung his head and climbed up the steps of the train and back into the cold domain of their most recent oppressors.

●

After some delay, during which damages were assessed and emergency repairs were made, the train continued its slow, deliberate trek westward towards Germany. As it swayed and lurched down the tracks through the forest, those on board now had the opportunity to either grieve their loss or thank God for sparing their lives.

Daria, Iwan, and Petro huddled in a far corner of the train, quietly talking over the day's events. While they would be forever grateful and awestruck that their family was again spared, that they had survived yet another near death experience, they couldn't help but voice their anxiety and to question how many more close calls they could narrowly escape.

CHAPTER 16

Only Luckier

It was early November 1944. The clatter of the train had slowed, then ceased altogether. We had reached our destination. We were in the southern part of Germany, in a town called Immenstadt, near Kempten Allgau, which is about twenty-five miles west of München, not far from the Austrian border.

The seemingly endless staccato of the train wheels was replaced by the voices of the Germans yelling for all arrivals to disembark and receive their instructions for housing. Our family was assigned to stay at a German guesthouse for a few days, then to a railway stationmaster's cabin for an indefinite duration.

This cabin, which was really more of a hut, was built for one person, but it soon became home to our family of five, as well as to three other men—strangers to both us and to each other. Sleeping at the end of each day's work became a very creative process.

All the men, including Iwan and Petro, were assigned to work loading and unloading boxcars. All laborers were issued certificates, which could be redeemed for food rations. As a bonus, if a carton was accidentally shattered, the contents of the food could be gathered and claimed by the laborers. The German supervisors paid little attention to such practices and probably shared in these spoils for their own families as well. Often, Iwan and Petro would come 'home' with their pockets weighed down with apples or canned goods. These goods became ingredients for the barter system, or as they referred to it back then, the 'Black Market,' whereby, whenever possible, workers would exchange products from German civilians for goods that they needed. Because of the long war, the German civilians were also in need of adequate food so they eagerly made such exchanges. Especially missed were 'luxury' items such as tea, coffee, sugar, flour, canned specialties, and fruit. These items were happily exchanged for more basic items like eggs, butter, fat back, poultry, and other meats. Displaced persons like us had done without for so long that 'basic' had become 'luxury.'

COMPARED TO the poor living conditions in other German labor camps, these were bearable and possibly even an improvement over those in which the Zapar family had previously existed. There was a strong roof over their heads and walls that kept the biting winds at bay.

Days turned into weeks and it became easier and easier to regard the camp more as a place of employment than a prison. Iwan and Petro had figured out the system enough to continue not only to bring home food for their family but to replenish the supply in their trunk as well. For the most part, all of the refugees were thankful to have decent accommodations and the opportunity to work for their families, taking their *wages* in the form of food and shelter.

During the weeks that they stayed in the trainmaster's hut they were able to let their guards down, if only slightly. It was a strange thing that seemed to be happening to this young family, including Petro. When you constantly face life and death decisions and your world feels so out of control, you begin trying to control anything that you possibly can. They had been living in fear and devastation for so long that now, when they woke up in the morning, they didn't see another day, they saw hope. When they saw one of the German guards, they didn't see evil but rather opportunity. Life had changed so drastically for them that they couldn't waste a single minute feeling sorry for themselves or bemoaning their situation. All they could do was make the most of it. And they did.

Although growing increasingly round, Daria found she enjoyed cleaning the trainmaster's quarters. It took her mind off of the war and gave her pride when the men came home each evening and noticed that she'd tidied up the place.

Iwan and Petro began to talk about things other than life and death choices that had to be made. They began to allow themselves to reminisce about their childhood times. They even giggled once as they tried to recollect their fluent *Talabarske*.

Lesio and Lyiubchyk once again had green grass and fields in which to run and to their delight they could even find some spots to build their hidden forts. But still, life couldn't help but take its toll on all of them. Their faces were becoming prematurely weathered due to the extreme conditions in which they lived and their skin had taken on an unnatural hue due to their recent lack of sunlight and malnutrition. But right now, as best they could tell, they were all happy. They knew life could be short. To live in the moment felt almost selfish or even a tad naïve, but that is exactly what they did.

Even Petro began to relax. And a couple of the single ladies in the camp caught his eye.

•

What remained the constant reminder that there was still a war raging was the frequency of alert sirens warning of bombing attacks by the Allied forces. They became regular, if not daily, occurrences. When these alarms were wailing, there wasn't much anyone could do other than to seek shelter wherever they could find it.

When the family initially arrived, Iwan, Daria, and Petro would take the boys, evacuate the little hut, and run into the nearby hills at the first shriek of the air siren. But after doing this for days and weeks, over and over again, they became complacent, as did all the prisoners of the camp. It eventually became habit to stop, remain as still and silent as possible, and carefully listen to see if they could gauge the distance of the strikes by the sound. Having been through it before, they certainly knew the sound of an impending attack.

As time went by and as the alarm sounded with greater frequency, there were even times that they would wait out the raid and not leave the hut at all.

One night, just as the sun had fully set, they all lay down in their usual puzzle piece fashion in an attempt to stay warm. Lyiubchyk was always cold and had figured a way to saddle up against his mama, with Lesio on the other side of him, and to tuck his arms into his shirt, mummy style, then lay on his stomach, sealing in as much heat as possible. He had just settled into this odd little package when the air strike warning sounded. No one flinched. Barely anyone paid much attention either. Iwan began to roll over lackadaisically but something caught him in his stomach. His eyes popped open. He lay there for another second then abruptly stood up.

"We need to go. Everyone up! I don't know why or what for, but this one just feels different. Let's go," he insisted.

"Are you sure, brother?" Petro asked groggily.

"Well, no, I'm not sure." Then his voice became more forceful. "But let's go. C'mon. Up! Let's get out of here."

In a second, all five of them, plus the other three men that were sharing the accommodations, were on their feet with their shoes on and out the door. And, as they typically did, the brothers grabbed the trunk and began running with it. They ran into the cold night air to their usual spot on the hill, behind a tree that overlooked the encampment.

Quietly, they waited, more annoyed than anxious about any impending danger. Since they were already out the door and sitting on the cold ground, they figured at this point they might as well wait it out until the alarms were silenced. They could see their breath as they exhaled and the bitter cold was beginning to settle into their bones. As all children do, the boys grew bored and cold and began to ask when they could go back.

Iwan still looked pensive and Petro was watching in his peripheral for a signal from him that they could return.

Finally, with the alarms still sounding but nothing happening, Petro got to his feet. "This is crazy. I'm heading back. Brother, it's done. Nothing's happening—"

No sooner had he finished speaking that last syllable than the biggest explosion they had ever seen or heard struck the camp.

A ball of blue and orange flames came hurtling out of the sky and quickly engulfed the huts. Within seconds the heat channeled up the hill. All eight of their faces were buried in the dirt as they threw their hands behind their heads and pushed themselves down into the earth as hard as they could.

Daria struggled to find a position that she felt would protect her, the child growing inside of her, and the boys, but finally she just threw one of her arms around her sons as best she could, pressing one ear to the earth and covering the other with her free hand. A minute passed and it didn't seem as if any more bombs would be falling from the sky. Down below from where they lay, they could hear terrified shrieks and the crackling of fire. The stench of burning wood, gas, and flesh infused the damp evening air.

The sirens were still sounding but the raid seemed to have died down. They got to their feet and, one next to the other, stared down from the hill at what had been their most recent *home*. The whole area was lit up and they quickly saw that the bombing had been closer this time than it had ever been before.

The flashes from the residual explosions seemed to be coming from the general direction of the railroad tracks and, once again, not wanting to risk the safety of the family, they had to sit things out on the hill. They piled up, on, and around each other in an attempt to keep warm, and got whatever sleep they could remotely come by as they waited out the night.

When the first light of dawn crept through the trees and awoke them, they began to make their way back down to the camp. Their hearts ached in their chests as they took in the scale of destruction. Twisted and mangled train tracks entangled in haphazardly strewn boxcars dotted the landscape for as far as their eyes could see. Fires smoldered and the devastation was rampant. Many of the other prisoners who had survived were equally stunned and walked in circles not knowing what to do. They held whatever clothing they could find over their noses and mouths to help keep the incessant smoke from filling their lungs.

When Daria and Iwan got to the trainmaster's hut, their hearts sank yet again. It was demolished. Nothing was left, other than ashes and a few pieces of strewn boards. Again, many lives were lost. Petro and Iwan went about their duty to humankind, quickly transforming themselves into grave-diggers and priests.

Later that evening as they were huddled in their makeshift lodging, Daria looked at Iwan and, in front of Petro and the boys, asked very bluntly, "How did you know?"

"Huh? What? How did I know what, my dear?" Iwan was too exhausted to think, much less speak.

"Of all the times for us to heed the call of the sirens how did you know that was going to happen last night? To me, they sounded like they always do. Why were those different?" she begged.

"I don't know. I honestly don't know." Iwan stared off into the distance. "It wasn't so much that I had the answer, as it was something guiding me. I don't know if it was God, or an angel, or just that voice that says things in the back of your head. Whoever, or whatever, it was, saved our lives."

Then he looked down at Lyiubchyk and Lesio and said very sternly and with great emphasis, "Boys, please always remember this. Just because we are still living while others have died before our eyes does not mean that we are any smarter than they were. All it means is that we are luckier. Don't ever forget that."

CHAPTER 17

Repatriation

Since our hut was destroyed, we received permission to move into the barracks. Group housing was assigned on the basis of nationality, primarily to facilitate interpretation of work assignments to the laborers by German supervisors. We remained in those barracks for several weeks until distressing word was received that an agreement had been reached by the Allied Forces to allow the Soviet Russian government to forcibly return all displaced persons to their homeland. This practice was called 'repatriation.' Although this gesture was naively perceived by the Allied powers as a humanitarian effort on the part of the Soviets, every displaced person correctly understood the true intent for their return.

The displaced persons would be herded, loaded on board trains, and returned for what would be certain execution by the Communist Army as traitors. Upon word of this repatriation, many chose not to be returned—by committing suicide. Some jumped out of windows, others cut their own wrists, and some just intentionally fled knowing they would be shot and killed in a quick, and somewhat humane manner.

UPON HEARING THE news of repatriation, Iwan, Daria, and Petro all became increasingly distraught. It seemed as though their luck was about to run out. On an hourly basis they heard the shrieks of their neighbors trying to flee or came across bodies covered with flimsy cloth, lined up to be disposed of. It was a dark few days and it was hard for them not to lose their minds.

Petro, Iwan, and Daria tried to come up with answers. They were filled day and night with anguish and turmoil over not having better solutions. They just knew death was not the answer. They would fight it to its bitter end, just as they had sworn in their pact to each other years earlier.

The next couple of nights Daria lay next to Lyiubchyk and Lesio as they slept, trying to muffle her sobbing. Her heart broke every time she looked at the two of them. Although she tried to stifle it, her mind would wander as it imagined all the horrible things that could happen to them. She thought of that night that Iwan and Petro left their own mother and father and how heartbroken their mother must have been the next day to know that in all likelihood she had seen the last of her sons. Daria's hand was cupped over her bosom, upon her heart. She felt that if she pressed her breast hard enough then maybe she could keep her heart from jumping out of her chest. A moment later she slowly brought her hand down to her abdomen to feel the baby inside of her, twisting and turning.

"Oh, little one," she thought. "I am so sorry that we are bringing you into a world like this. It's not what I ever imagined and it's not what I ever wanted for you. The more you grow inside of me the more I see of this evil world and the more doubt surfaces as to how you will ever survive this." Daria lifted her head slightly to see Iwan and Petro—their shoulders moved up and down in heavy breathing—before continuing with her inner monologue. "Aye, aye, aye. Just know that you are loved. And I know if we survive this, there will be more love for you and Lyiubchyk and Lesio than any three children can imagine. You will grow up strong—because you will have to—but I promise you that you will know love. Fortunately, inside me you have been shielded from the hate that is raining down on us, but I hope for you that you will never see or remember any of this."

•

As the new dawn greeted the refuges, Iwan awoke with a plan. He grabbed Lyiubchyk and headed out to the barracks.

"Daria, Petro, I'll be back. Lyibuchyk and I have something to do."

Then he glanced Daria's way and said, "Don't worry. He'll be safe with me. You two stay here with Petro."

After they got a good distance from the barracks, he pulled Lyiubchyk behind one of the buildings, out of the scrutiny of the guards, and, kneeling down next to his son, began to act as if he was rolling Lyiubchyk's pants legs up to keep them from getting muddied. Softly yet solemnly he spoke.

"Now Lyiubchyk, you listen to me, okay?"

"Yes, Father," Lyiubchyk respectfully bowed his head.

"Lyiubchyk, this is very serious. You must do as I tell you. Don't ask questions right now but please do as I say."

He began to rub Lyiubchyk's cheeks so vigorously they began to sting. To get even more blood flowing to them he began to softly smack at them. Lyiubchyk bit his lip, trying not to ask questions and do as he was told.

"Now listen. Here's what I need you to do. We are going to walk right over there to that guard in that office. Do you see whom I am talking about Lyiubcyk? Do you see him?"

"Yes, Father," he obediently replied.

"Quickly we are going to walk over to him. I will do all the talking. Don't say a word but what I need you to do is to look very sick. Cough a little bit, but don't be obvious. Lyiubchyk, I am counting on you. Our entire family—Lesio, Mama, and Uncle Petro—are *all* counting on you. You must act but you must not overact. Does that make sense? Let me see how you will do that. Show me."

Lyiubchyk did his best impression of illness and, fortunately, it was spot on. He interjected just the right amount of coughing while at the same time wearing a forlorn but not overly histrionic expression.

"Perfect! Now rub your eyes, *rub them hard*…and let's go."

Iwan grabbed Lyiubchyk in his arms and did some of his own acting. He gathered his pace and he burst in the office, wearing the anguished look that had become all too customary over these past several years.

"Officer! Officer! You must help me, please. My child, Lyiubchyk, he is very sick."

Again, Lyiubchyk perfectly played his part as Iwan pressed his hand to his son's forehead pretending to feel for a fever.

"He's been sick for days and isn't recovering. He's been in and out of sleep and mostly incoherent. We thought his fever would break by now but it has not. Please, what can you do for us? Is there a doctor? Is there something that can be done? Please, I beg of you."

The officer looked at the child and then back to Iwan. Iwan's thick legs seemed to be affixed to the floorboards. He didn't want to move. He didn't want to show any lessening of his fear for his son's health. The officer began to speak unexcitedly. "Well, sir. I can see that your child is very ill.

However, so are many children and laborers like yourself for that matter. Surely you must know that we do not have doctors who will be able to attend to either one of you, right?"

"Well, I had hoped..." Iwan played along, actually relieved that this was the officer's reply. He didn't want to risk a German doctor examining Lyiubchyk and turning them in for lying about his health.

"Right! You had hoped. Well, I'm sorry to inform you that we do not presently have the staff for your kind. So you will have to take your son back to the barracks to wait out his condition."

Pleadingly, and this time his facial expression didn't need to be faked, Iwan looked deep into the guardsman's eyes, trying to pierce his soul, if indeed he had one. "Sir, please. I know there must be something that can be done. There is so much sickness in the barracks and I believe that he has not been able to get better on account of that. Please, sir. What can you do? I fear for his life."

The officer looked back down at his desk, this time shaking his head while exhaling irritably.

By this time Lyiubcyhk was pretending to be asleep but his little heart was pounding inside his chest.

The officer slid a drawer open and pulled out what looked to be an official form of some sort. Grabbing his pen, he hurriedly scribbled his signature on the bottom of it and handed it over to Iwan.

"Here. This is all I can do. It is a certificate that says any German family with extra living space must take in your family under temporary residency. I can't promise that you will find anyone who will admit to having extra living space and I can't say how long they will allow you to stay if they do admit it. But it gets you out of here and can perhaps provide your son a chance to get better. This is the best I can do."

Iwan instantly exhaled a sigh of relief. "Thank you, kind sir. I know my son, Lyiubchyk, and our family will be so grateful to you for this. May I please ask you one more question?"

"What?" The guard blurted, annoyed.

"I have no idea where we are or in what direction to head. Any suggestions? I don't want to walk further than I have to with my dear Lyiubchyk in this condition."

The soldier's agitation seemed to soften a bit as he stood up from his chair and pointed out the window.

"See that hill over there? There's a mountain directly behind it. There could be a farmer that may have possible accommodations for you. If I were you, that's the direction I would head."

And with that the soldier abruptly took his seat again and began rifling through his stack of paperwork as if to say, *You can leave now.*

With certificate in hand, Iwan, still holding Lyiubchyk in his arms, backed his way out of the door, nodding one final time to the soldier, as Lyiubchyk stared, glassy-eyed, at that eagle pin on the gentlemen's uniform.

•

Back in the barracks, the family wasted no time preparing to leave behind the chaos of the camp. While they felt an incredible sense of regret for those that had no other option than repatriation, they couldn't risk their own extinction just to assuage their feelings of guilt. And deep down, they knew any other family would do the same thing they were doing had they devised their own plan sooner.

With just the clothes on their backs and the family trunk, they made their way out of the compound and over the hill. Eventually, the mountain the guard had spoken of came into view. Given Daria's condition they had to stop often, but these were welcome reprieves for them all as there were many impediments along the hills and trails. Iwan and Petro weren't feeling all that great on the hike and could barely fathom how Daria and the boys were making it as expediently as they were. This family was a force to be reckoned with.

After a day's hike up the mountain they arrived on the outskirts of a picturesque little town called Blaichach. There they found a typical Bavarian homestead, owned by one Herr Maier. Blaichach sat in a small valley below the lower peak they had just crested. The Maier home was situated near the village church which had a steeple so high it could be seen from nearly anywhere in the whole town. The mountain was still snow-capped but a winter's worth of ice had defrosted and was busy swelling the streams that flowed through town.

Initially, when they came across the Maier house, they were reluctant to go up to the door. But they knew they must, and, armed with the certificate, Iwan and Petro made their way up the worn front stoop while Daria and the boys waited a short distance behind them but within clear eyesight of whoever might answer.

Upon hearing the knock, Herr Maier opened the door. Rigidly, Iwan and Petro stood before him not knowing what to expect from this stranger—and they assumed he felt the same way.

After a brief pause, Iwan very concisely explained to him their situation. He didn't want to say too much, for fear they would be turned in for repatriation, so he mostly let the certificate do the talking.

Herr Maier and his wife were not particularly thrilled with the request to have five other people living with them but, with the certificate as proof that they wouldn't be acting illegally—shielding strangers who were running from the law, and seeing Daria that far along in her pregnancy, they conceded and allowed the five refugees to live in the storage area of their home—also known as the barn.

There was no heat in the barn and the family used hay and pine to make themselves palettes to sleep on each night. Fortunately for them, there were no livestock living in the barn at the time, only chickens that ran around outside.

Given that it was now March, the stinging cold of the Bavarian winter had begun to subside. Any discomfort the Zapars experienced paled in comparison to the alternate predicament of those being repatriated to the Soviets.

•

The room was cold and damp. Iwan and Petro had taken the boys out to the fields so that they couldn't hear their mother's screams as her labor progressed. As painful as the delivery was, Daria found there was something incredibly healing in it, even as she screamed and cursed through the pain. Having been through labor twice before, she knew what to expect and, while it was horrifically painful without the aid of modern medicine, she was happy to go through the ebb and flow of the contractions and to bring this new life into the world. Finally, on March 24, 1945, Daria delivered a little girl, Zweneslava, or *Zvinusia* as she was lovingly called.

CHAPTER 18

Children in a Parallel World

**Daria, Lesio and Lyiubchyk holding the months
old Zvinusia in Blaichack, Germany.**
Photo courtesy of the Zapar family.

*We stayed in the spartan, lice-infested conditions of the Maier home
for several months. The war had essentially wound itself down by this
time—May of 1945. Not only did our sojourn in Blaichach allow*

Mama to regain her strength from childbirth, but it also allowed the postwar dynamics and political climate a chance to unfold.

The rebuilding of the bombed cities and infrastructure had begun, and those like us who had survived would need to begin their own rebuilding. The unimaginable horrors of war were coming to an end as Nazi Germany was defeated, but, as a residual effect, the German citizenry shared its own defeat from the toll of the war—both physically and mentally. It was still a very dark time.

The end of World War II brought only partial relief to all who survived. Many cities had been reduced to indistinguishable rubble— roads, bridges, and railways were destroyed. Death camps and slave labor camps were liberated but its survivors needed to be cared for. Those who perished needed to be buried in mass graves to prevent the spread of diseases. Needs were dire at every turn.

UPON HEARING that the war had concluded, Iwan and Petro set about trying to make enough money to find more stable housing for the family. Because there were so many refugees and concentration camp survivors melded together in this postwar existence, everyone was looking for a job and everyone was trying to scrape together whatever coins they could to ultimately put a roof over their family's heads. This made jobs hard to come by—and money even harder. Townspeople were happy to barter food for work but all Germans had been hit hard and money was tight in this new economy.

Fortunately, there were Allied goods and services beginning to stream in to help not only rebuild the nation but also to restore civilian life to some semblance of order. In the midst of living without so many basic human needs, life continued on for those lucky enough to still be counted among the living.

As would be expected among those such as the Zapar family, who had done without for so long, there developed a natural human *hierarchy* of needs, in which less urgent requirements came to seem like frivolities. And the desire for these *frivolities*, formerly considered necessities, was therefore suppressed.

During this time, Iwan and Petro were fortunate enough to find *jobs* helping the Allied forces. Every day they would go to the nearest railroad station and unload trains. It was backbreaking labor and it frequently began shortly after sunrise. As the day crept on they would continue the nearly automated motion of grabbing, twisting, and delivering the packages to the next person standing in assembly-line fashion behind them. With very little sustenance and upwards of nine or ten hours of continual labor, Iwan and Petro found themselves constantly tired and nearly whittled down to nothing. But they hardly noticed, as they were so grateful to be able to work towards removing their family from the inadequate conditions in the Maier barn.

In this new economy, Iwan and Petro would show up every morning and take their orders from the Allied soldiers as to which trains needed to be unloaded or what *job positions* needed filling. In return, they would receive not money, but rather, certificates that were redeemable at various Allied aid stations.

The Maier family had been generous enough to pass along scraps of food that they were not using for themselves, such as potato peelings. Daria would then turn the potato peelings and whatever else they could scavenge into soup. By this point, she came to pride herself on her ability to make soup out of just about anything.

But becoming increasingly tired of making do with Daria's creative recipes from the scraps they received, Iwan and Petro started their own *black market*, utilizing a system put in place by the Allied forces. And they weren't the only ones to use it. Everyone knew it was going on and, since the government did not control this barter system, it was very much illegal. It was a constant risk to take, but in the brother's eyes it was yet another necessary evil of their existence—they would do whatever they had to do to keep their young family alive.

Just as Petro and Iwan had helped their respective general stores thrive through their business savvy and knack for figuring out not just how to make money, but also how to grow a business, they began to figure out ways to make a quick profit from this system. They weren't proud of their efforts but they knew that this was what they must do not only to get their family fed, but also to get them out of the barn and into a place where a solid roof would be over their heads.

When they went to redeem their hard-earned work certificates for food, Iwan and Petro would spend their time wisely, carefully choosing their items. They would start by taking the bare minimum of what they needed for their family's survival. They had to keep the children growing and Daria in robust enough health to continue breastfeeding Zvinusia. But bare minimum was now *extreme* bare minimum. They all had to sacrifice a little comfort to properly skim off the system.

After they chose the items most needed by the family they would move on to the items that were scarce due to wartime rationing. These items were especially precious in rural areas of Germany such as the one in which they currently found themselves. High on the list of desirable and scarce items were coffee, sugar, tea, flour, chocolate, soaps, and personal care products. The brothers would choose as many of these much-coveted items as their certificates afforded them and then they would go out into the countryside and try to either barter them for more of their staples—such as milk, bacon, chicken, apples, and other basic goods for the home—or they would sell them at a drastically reduced rate compared to what would be charged at the village shops.

Since Daria was mostly left at the barn to take care of Zvinusia, Lesio and Lyiubchyk would often accompany their father and uncle on these *black market* errands. Iwan and Petro took turns using an old rusty bicycle that they had bartered some labor for—one of the boys would ride along on the handlebars. The job of the boys was to hold the backpack loaded down with the items for trade and to help provide the façade of an unassuming father and an innocent son picnicking together rather than that of a duo making the rounds and illegally engaging in black market business transactions.

Even though they were being used to cover up what was really going on, and even though Iwan and Petro involved them in the shady dealings as innocent accomplices, the boys enjoyed having their father and uncle all to themselves and, while it was no picnic, they were proud to bring home what they had helped to acquire after the deals were completed. It was very fulfilling for them all and after months of back and forth trading it became lucrative enough for them to be able to leave behind the meager barn for a more secure shelter and life.

•

In addition to the day-to-day dealings on the black market and prior to their departure from the village of Blaichach, Lyiubchyk and Lesio enjoyed running the streets of their little town. After being cooped up in unbearable conditions in painfully small surroundings, the streets of this new post-war Germany were both exhilarating and menacing for the now five- and seven-year-old boys. There was a small park where they were often allowed to wander off and play. One Saturday, the men were offloading cargo at the train station and the boys were there by themselves. They were having a ball, romping around on what was left of the timeworn play area that consisted of a couple of swings and slides.

It was a fairly warm spring day—not a cloud was in the pristine blue sky—and many other villagers were milling around the freshly sprung daffodils and tulips that lined the perimeter of the park. The scent of spring clung to the lilac trees. Teenagers were practicing the fine art of falling in love and even a few of the adults were playing hooky from life's obligations. Lyiubchyk and Lesio were on opposite ends of the park from each other, which wasn't an uncommon occurrence. After living in such tight quarters for so long, every chance either of them got they went in opposite directions—not out of frustration with each other but, rather, just because they could.

While pausing briefly at the top of the slide, Lesio saw a small group of people gathering a short distance away from where he was. He could hear the yelling of a German man but, of course, he didn't have a clue what he was saying. He could hear the agitation in the dialect and, even at Lesio's young age, he could tell that this man was not mentally stable. He was hysterical and what Lesio could not understand then but later found out, was that he was a German soldier who was experiencing what would be known today as post-traumatic stress disorder. The man was lamenting Germany's lost war and his part in it. Curious, Lesio slid down the slide and made his way to the outskirts of the crowd. Not a moment later the man's speech came to a halt. There was an eerie and tense silence, and then, nearly as abruptly as the speech had ended, he pulled a machine gun from his coat and began to fire—a burst of bullets flew into the crowd.

Instinctively and from what he'd learned from his own history, Lesio threw himself down on the ground, paralyzed and gripped with fear. From behind the crazed madman's back, one brave onlooker jumped out and wrestled the man down on the dirt. Another threw himself upon the rifle and began to pry it out of the man's hands. Chaos ensued as shouts and screams erupted from the crowd. All Lesio could think was, "Where is Lyiubchyk? Please brother, be safe."

Lifting his head just enough to be able to see the flat horizon over the blades of grass, he scanned left to right looking for his brother. He still dared not move since he didn't know if the assault was completely over, if the man had been subdued. He put his head back down, now feeling a lump in his throat and a pain in his chest. Seconds seemed to tick on for minutes but he was paralyzed, not knowing what to do or where his brother was. The perfumed air was now mixed with that recognizable smell of gun smoke.

He felt someone nudge him on his left side but still he dared not look up for fear it was the madman. He felt more nudging and then he felt a body lie down next to him—an arm wrapped itself over his back and grabbed onto his shoulder. "Lesio! Brother, are you okay?" a small voice whispered in his ear.

"Lyiubchyk?"

"Yes! It's me, brother! I thought you were dead!"

"...And I thought you were dead, Lyiubchyk."

"What happened? I don't understand. One minute I was on the swings and the next minute someone grabbed me and threw me to the ground. I don't even know who it was" Lyiubchyk said. "I never did see them."

Lyiubchyk then listened as Lesio quickly told him how he'd experienced the melee from the slide and from the out-skirts of the gathered crowd. Then he patted Lesio's shoulder. "C'mon, brother. We need to go. We are both okay. That's all that matters. If Mama finds out about what just happened here before we are back home safe, I'm afraid she will have a heart attack."

They both got to their feet and, without wasting a second, darted out of the park towards home. Even years later they would often wonder about how they made it out unscathed and, sadly, they would also wonder how many people had been stricken by the mad man's bullets. They would never know the answer to either of those questions but they would always firmly believe that a guardian angel of some sort was looking over them. For the rest of his life, Lyiubchyk would often strain to make out the face of the person that had grabbed him off the swing and threw him to the ground. The face never came to Lyiubchyk. But the sense of gratitude he felt towards this stranger never waned.

•

Upon reaching their house, they discovered that the news had traveled faster than they'd anticipated—Daria was already in a heightened state of panic. She had convinced herself that the boys were both dead. Once they walked into the barn, she scooped them up in her arms and broke down—tears streamed down her worry-worn face. A thousand times she cursed towards the heavens but a thousand times more she hugged both boys tightly, smoothed their hair, and thanked God.

"It's okay, Lesio. It's okay, Lyiubchyk. Mama is here. I'm so sorry you had to see that. I am so sorry you will have to live with that memory. There are so many memories I wish I were able to erase from your sweet, precious little minds. So much I wish we could do over. I wish I could have been there to protect you. I am so thankful that the heavens were watching over you today and that you are here with me. *Ya tebe lyublyu.* I love you."

CHAPTER 19

Development

ДО КАНАДІЙСЬКИХ УКРАЇНЦІВ.

Українська родина, яку бачите на висше поданій фотографії, а яка перебуває тепер на скитальщині в Німеччині, просить канадійських українців, щоби забрали їх з країни голоду, терпіння і непевности до Канади. Родина працьовита — рільники.

Один, або кількох багатих фармерів зложіться на подорож, виробіть афідейвит і поможіть їм сюди приїхати, а Всевишний винагородить вас за те сторицею. І родина буде вам завсіди вдячна. А що ви дасьте, те вона вам відробить.

Сумківці якої будь округи по фармах — влаштуйте представлення, концерти на ту ціль. Одіж, що на них, то нині ціле їх майно.

Тих, що заінтересуються і схочуть та зможуть прийти з допомогою, прошу зголошуватися по близші інформації до:

Steve Peleshok,

539 Elliee Ave.,   Winnipeg. Man.

**Actual appeal for sponsorship placed in
Ukrainian-Canadian Newspaper.**

Courtesy of the Zapar family.

Finally having saved up just enough money to be able to pay some form of rent, we left the Maier household and moved into the city of Kempten with a family by the name of Zimmerman. They operated a butcher shop downstairs and lived above the shop. There was an extra apartment down the hall from theirs, which they rented to us.

While we enjoyed a relatively safe and comfortable post-war existence in Kempten, Iwan decided to submit applications for all of us to emigrate from Germany to either America or Canada—whichever country accepted our petition first. Either country was fine with us, as each provided safety, normalcy, freedom, and, very importantly, the opportunity to mold one's future, limited only by a person's ambition and willingness to work hard to achieve success.

All the necessary papers were completed through the appropriate consulate. Approval for immigration to America was conditional on having a sponsor who agreed to provide temporary food and lodging and assurance of employment. The fee for transoceanic travel at that time was approximately 700 US dollars, which was a huge sum in those days. However, Catholic Relief organizations had volunteered assistance to those seeking to emigrate, with the understanding that this sum would be repaid to them as soon as possible. This would, of course, depend on the émigré's level of employment and general financial status. This could be the break our family needed to distance our self from our terrible post-war world! We were eagerly waiting to be notified of a sponsor. Father even had a family photo taken, which was posted in an American and Ukrainian-Canadian newspaper, petitioning for a sponsor. All that was left to do now was wait, pray, and be patient.

FOR THE FIRST time in an immeasurable number of years, the family began to feel the noose of war loosening and, even though they knew they were not bound to take firm hold, they began to put roots down in Kempten, settling into their tiny apartment.

The Zapars lived directly down the hall from Frau Zimmerman and, as they got to know her, they became very close friends. Having never seen her husband, they would eventually come to find out that he was still being held as a German prisoner of war and was biding his time in who knows what kinds of conditions while Frau Zimmerman was left behind to take care of their two children, a son named Boldel and a daughter named Anelise. Frau Zimmerman was very kind. She had a stoic disposition and a huge heart—constantly bringing Daria almost-expired meat up from her butcher shop. Frau Zimmerman, too, knew the pangs of hunger that lasted long past the war's end. She fought hard throughout the war to keep her own family fed and to keep the shop open as she watched the continual march of the Nazi regime back and forth in front of her shop windows. In the same way that Iwan and Petro's mother and father had become human pawns in this war so, too, had her husband.

In addition to tending to the store and her children, Frau Zimmerman had the responsibility of taking care of her elderly father who had an advanced form of dementia. Members of the Zapar family would often walk out of their door to venture downstairs, only to find themselves face to face with this aging man. Most of the time he would be standing there, stark naked. Lesio and Lyiubchyk would look at the floor and giggle. Daria would blush and try her absolute hardest to pretend she didn't see Frau Zimmerman's father's naked body. Iwan and Petro, on the other hand, when confronted with such a scene, would gingerly grab the old man by his elbows and shuffle him either in the direction of the bathroom or back to the safe confines of his own apartment.

So many times Iwan and Petro felt that they themselves were going crazy. They always felt fortunate to have the gentle guidance of each other and of Daria to get them to their own safe shelter in the midst of their stormy world. They knew this man had probably suffered some of the same worries and setbacks that they, too, had been through and were in awe of how anyone could survive to such an advanced age during these times. They always had the utmost respect for the elderly and did not take lightly their turn to give back to those who had raised gentle, kind, and compassionate human beings such as Frau Zimmerman.

The boys had new playmates and they all ran the streets of Kempten together. Besides the joy of new friendship, an additional benefit was safety in numbers. It was finally getting easier for Daria to take care of Zvinusia and sometimes both mother and daughter would join the boys on their excursions.

Iwan and Petro found whatever manual labor or retail jobs they could, for however many hours a day it required to keep the roof over their heads and their family fed. They continued their black market dealings for some extra money on the side, too. Petro was able to find fairly stable employment in a small store again, checking inventories and trying his hardest to make the little shop thrive.

For the first time in so many years Iwan, Petro and Daria could begin to think about the future and the hopeful dream of stability and safety for their family. Since the late 1800's, Ukrainians had immigrated to America, mostly in response to advertisements seeking work in the mines of Pennsylvania— based on the promise of prosperity and earnings many times greater than they could have ever hoped for in Ukraine. So after hearing of waves of displaced Ukrainians already reaching this Promised Land, America became their first choice for shelter from the tyranny they had so long endured. And even though they knew they would never return to their beloved country while under Soviet rule, it was easiest to let go if they could regard America as a temporary home. So it was with much anxiety, focus and fortitude that they began to forge ahead with their plans.

Iwan worked in a photo lab and found he had a natural knack for photography. While preparing the family's documentation for a sponsor to get them to America—or Canada as their back up, and as far away from the grips of communism as possible—Iwan was able to barter some of his additional time in the shop in exchange for one family photo of the six of them that he could use to hopefully tug at the heartstrings of a stranger across the Atlantic.

By all accounts, the day the family went in to pose for this photograph was quite a day for them all. They were going to get a photo taken. A photo! Had this not been bartered from Iwan's service to the shop it would never have happened. A frivolous thing like a photograph was surely trumped by the needs of day-to-day existence such as food, clothes that were quickly outgrown, and the need to ensure the stability of renting Frau Zimmerman's extra room. He also knew that the opportunity to include a photo in their ad could not be ignored. For the same reason that Iwan was able to make Daria's father's general store thrive he was able to *sell* his own family. He had a natural knack for marketing and knew that this photo would provide the family the additional and needed means to have someone, anyone, feel a twinge of compassion and to sponsor them. A photo would be rare for other families like his, and, even though he felt bad, they had gone through too much and gotten too far to give it all up in order to keep things amongst fellow refugees *fair*. There was an unspoken rule among them all to do what you have to do to get your family *fed and fled*.

So here they were, the six of them, feeling completely normal—even a tad *ritzy*—arriving at the photography studio to find the man behind the camera waiting for them. They had all been able to round up halfway decent clothes. The men and the boys had slicked their hair back and Lesio and Lyiubchyk had put on their best-collared sweaters—ones that didn't have holes in them yet from their daily fort construction. Iwan and Petro looked very handsome in their suits. Iwan's didn't fit him so well and for that reason the photographer had him sit down. But Petro looked tall and stunningly handsome as he wore the perfectly fitting and sharp suit that Frau Zimmerman had let him borrow from her father's closet.

Expertly, Daria brushed back her dark, naturally wavy hair, looking serious and with a sense of purpose. Zvinusia, too young to fully understand where they were and what they were doing, wore a smocked dress—a hand-me-down from Anelise—and a hint of a frown. The crunching sound of the flash burst into the air and the camera did its job of capturing the moment—this beautiful family was perched on the hopeful seat to freedom.

•

The next day, at work, Iwan took it upon himself to develop the photo. There before his eyes he watched as the negative began to transpose his family on to a piece of photo paper. Breathing in deep the soothing smell of the photo developer as he sloshed the tray back and forth, he watched in full anticipation as he saw all six of their faces softly appear. After he was satisfied that the photo was perfectly developed, he took the paper out of the tray and clipped it on the line to dry.

For a brief moment he closed his eyes and took a deep breath, holding it in and then deliberately and slowly exhaling. He allowed himself to think about how, for so many years, he had not one time given up hope that his family would stay together and make it through all of this. However, today, it felt like the first time since walking out the door of his childhood home, that this hopeful wanting was beginning to transform into something else, something more. And he felt this deep down in his gut. This feeling was nearly unrecognizable, but in looking at these six faces staring back at him from the piece of photo paper, he was beginning to feel that perhaps this hope was a bit more than stubborn optimism. His eternal hope had begun to change. It had become more of a faith, and now he was beginning to see his faith's fruits gradually becoming rooted in some kind of reality.

CHAPTER 20

The Naked Angel

While we were anxiously waiting to emigrate from Germany, we heard of a concerted effort being made by Soviet troops to round up any stray displaced persons who had come from Russia or Ukraine and repatriate them. In reality, this meant they would be returned and executed as traitors.

IT WAS A SUNDAY afternoon and the family had returned home from church. They had been able to find other Ukrainian war survivors such as themselves and they enjoyed the bittersweet camaraderie of those in their same predicament. A little Ukrainian church service was allowed in a spare room of a makeshift Greek Orthodox church not too far from where they were living, and these families were thankful to share in their common faith every week. It helped them get through the week.

It had become the Zapar family tradition to pack a little picnic and eat together in the park after church services ended. Having been so cold during their years of retreat from Ukraine, they all enjoyed basking in the sun on particularly warm days. Often, after the picnic, all six of them would do little more than lay side by side, face up in the grass, relishing the beauty of the afternoon and the cozy rays of the sun. *They were alive!*

On this particular Sunday they slowly walked back to their spartan housing after the picnic and began their Sunday afternoon chores of getting ready for the week ahead. Daria had just gotten Zvinusia down for her afternoon nap, Lyiubchyk was drawing a landscape from something he remembered at the park, and Lesio was constructing a corner fort out of an old chair and sheets from his bed. Exhausted from the sixty- to seventy-hour workweek they had just put in, and knowing the coming week would be equally taxing, Iwan and Petro took to their usual armchairs for a respite from the drudgery of life.

The window overlooking the busy street below was open and the curtains danced on the warm breeze whirling around the room. From where Petro sat, he began to hear the clanking of what sounded like soldiers' boots below. Then he heard voices. Due to the brothers' endless workweeks and complete immersion in German society, they both were becoming fairly fluent in the language. Petro began to piece together enough words to make out the inquiries of the soldiers. They were looking for any displaced persons that might be sheltered in the building.

In fear of being seen, Petro, who had by then signaled Iwan over to the window, peered out as best he could and surveyed what was going on below. He could see Frau Zimmerman speaking to the soldiers and could make out her firm *Nein* as she continued to shake her head back and forth. A few more words were exchanged, none of which the brothers could make out. Then their hearts leapt out of their chests as the soldiers turned quickly on their heels and opened the door to Frau Zimmerman's building. Petro could see Frau Zimmerman's look of helpless anxiety as she peered up towards their window.

Upon hearing the door slam and the looming sound of the soldiers' boots on the wooden stairs below, Petro and Iwan leapt up, abandoning their vigil by the windowsill and quickly grabbing the boys and Daria from the kitchen.

"Petro! You stay with Daria and the boys. You will be the second line of defense should anything happen. Do you understand?" Iwan reached into a hall closet and quickly shoved a hammer into his brother's grasp while grabbing an ax for himself. "Here! Do whatever you find you must if this door opens.

Lyiubchyk and Lesio, I want you to hide in this closet and do not open the door under *any* circumstances. Plug your ears and close your eyes.

Daria, we can't wake Zvinusia—I'm afraid that she will begin to cry. But Petro will be here to stand guard by her side. You know that he will not let anything happen to her. I want you to get in the closet with the boys and hold them tight. And I want you, too, to plug your ears. Do you understand?" Iwan demanded.

"Yes, Iwan," Daria heeded her husband's warning, as she always did. She had listened to him on so many occasions and found their lives spared each time so she trusted him beyond measure.

"And, Daria...pray. Hard," he quickly added.

"Petro," he slapped his brother on the back and squeezed his shoulder. "Petro, please stand just on the other side of the bedroom door and don't let anything happen to them. I know you won't, but be ready to fight and I will do the same."

With a fast turn and stifling his footsteps, Iwan grabbed a hatchet and crept slowly to their front door. As directed,

Daria and the boys huddled in the closet while Zvinusia slept, peacefully unaware of the impending danger. Petro stood in a fixed position just to the left of the bedroom door. His feet were firmly planted on the hard wood flooring as he held the hammer high above his head, paralyzed but ready to take aim at the soldiers if necessary.

In the same pose as his brother, Iwan stood firmly on one side of the front door with the hatchet raised high above his head. He softly pressed his ear to the door, straining to hear what was happening on the other side. His heart was racing as he heard the German officers coming up the stairs. Fear and the lactic acid building in his arms made it hard to hold the hatchet without trembling. But he didn't dare budge.

The footsteps grew closer and closer until he could nearly feel the officers on the other side of the door. The terror Iwan and his family were feeling was beginning to boil to the surface of each and every one of them as they collectively tried to remain calm, or, at least, to quiet the pounding in their chests.

Anticipating the first knock at the door, Iwan held his breath and tightened his muscles so that he would be ready to attack. But the moment of anticipation seemed to carry on longer than he thought possible. He pressed his ear even harder to the door, straining to hear the rustle of the soldiers' uniforms or their breath on the other side. He expected them to burst through at any second.

He inhaled deeply, clenching his ax and tightening every muscle in his body, when, all of a sudden he heard what sounded like the soldiers spinning on their heels and walking off. Their steps began to grow softer. They were moving away from the family's door. Not a second later, a third, barely audible set of footsteps could be heard coming down the hall.

"What the—" one of the soldiers said, adding a crass German slang word to his epithet.

"Can't a fellow go to the bathroom around here, ladies?" came the response. It was Frau Zimmerman's father! What Iwan & Petro couldn't see on the other side of the door, but had found out later was that he had waltzed up to the German soldiers fully nude. After his initial greeting he saw their weapons and threw himself to the floor. "Oh my God! Don't shoot! I swear I was only going to the bathroom. Surely you wouldn't shoot an old man just for trying to take a piss in his own house?" He remained with his hands over his head and his bare buttocks facing the soldiers, pressing himself down into the cold hallway floor.

The soldiers looked at him and felt pity for the poor German elder. One began to speak up with a slight air of agitation. "Sir, pick yourself up off the floor and by all means go take a piss. You may want to put some clothes on, though," he snickered. "Roaming the halls naked is no way for a man of your age to impress the ladies."

The other soldier laughed and the two men helped Frau Zimmerman's father off the floor—he then meandered into the bathroom.

After that, the soldiers made their way back down the stairs. Perhaps they felt it was just the loony old man who lived there and that's why he felt comfortable enough to walk around naked. Or maybe they were careless or hurried in carrying out their orders. And was the old man in a full state of dementia at the time anyway? Or was he perhaps trying to save the Zapar family's lives in return for all those times Petro and Iwan had so patiently ushered him back to his apartment?

No one, other than fate, would ever know for sure how or why this all played out as it did, but what was clear to them all was that at least one life was spared that day. One of those soldiers would surely have been dead—hacked to death by Iwan's hatchet or Petro's hammer—and perhaps six more lives would have been lost had that knock at their door occurred.

So, in another strange twist of the family's fate, Frau Zimmerman's father had become yet another one of their guardian angels, guiding their destiny through one more day. It was nearly impossible to fully comprehend, but they knew— and they would always remember—the day their guardian angel, their *naked* guardian angel, came down the hallway to take a piss. And for that, they were forever grateful.

CHAPTER 21

Bridge Collapse

Even in the worst of times, people yearn for fun and frivolity, the very things stolen from their lives by war. As a psychological relief from the postwar reconstruction of their lives, and, in an attempt to restore some semblance of order to their personal and family's lives, the German people tried to rekindle life as they remembered it before the horrors of the war befell them.

Even with the war having ended, life and survival could not be taken for granted. Perils existed in the most seemingly innocuous places. An element of risk, mixed with a healthy dose of caution, needed to always be a part of everyday life.

HAVING SURVIVED yet another close call, the family quickly pushed the scare back into their subconscious, as had become their wont in order to engage in a *normal* life and continue their day to day existence. Especially because they were a young family, it was necessary for each of them to get out of the house and into the fresh air if only to prevent stagnating in the apartment, living in constant fear of a soldier's knock.

Daria had become astute at finding out what free events were taking place in the town and would often find fairs and festivals that she could take the children to so that they could get a taste of what living should be about.

It was now the fall of 1946. On a particularly crisp and clear day Daria had gotten word of one such fair on the outskirts of town. It was the talk of the entire neighborhood and many of the families planned on hiking out to the fair together. While some of the activities would cost money that they didn't have, they could, at the very least, stand around and watch as those who did have money to spend at the fair enjoyed the games and rides.

Daria dressed Zvinusia and the boys and Iwan and Petro were able to take a few hours off from work to go, too. It seemed like this fair was the talk of the town and everyone was going to be there.

They made the twenty-minute trek to the outskirts of town and had only one final bridge to cross before getting to the open field where the fair was set up.

It was typical that many of the roads and bridges remained in states of disrepair, broken or destroyed by the Nazi army as they tore through the towns in retreat. The Nazis had nearly raped society of all its needs, making it next to impossible to function. But, in a postwar existence, if you chose to avoid the use of war-torn roads and bridges you would simply be restricted and quarantined to a gerbil-cage-sized corner of living space—or at least to one small town.

The particular bridge that the hopeful revelers needed to cross was heavily damaged but still very much standing and utilized on a daily basis. The throng of festival-goers made their way across it but nobody noticed the heavy sigh it was making under their weight.

Just before crossing, Lyiubchyk and Lesio spotted heaping piles of discharged weapons below the bridge and quickly fell behind as the four other family members began to make their way to the other side.

During war, it was customary for defeated armies to throw their weapons off bridges and into the water below, rendering them useless as they began to rust. Literally thousands of tarnished and corroded armaments lay by the water's edge and, just like any typical young boys, Lesio and Lyiubchyk were fascinated anytime they spotted such stocks. They quickly veered from crossing the bridge with their parents and made their way instead down to the edge of the water to pick up the discharged rifles.

Lyiubchyk picked one up and began to pretend to shoot Lesio with it. Lesio fell down in play, rolling over and quickly grabbing another to return attack on his brother. Lesio held one of the weapons in his right arm in perfect form, imitating the soldiers he'd watched on numerous occasions. He took aim at a nearby twig and pensively lined up the sight. Although a tad rusted in places, he was able to slowly squeeze the trigger until he was rewarded with the *click*. Fortunately, no bullets were discharged.

Lyiubchyk was in his own world, fondling the guns and admiring the sleek lines and cold steel lettering that he was hoping to recreate on his sketchpad when he got home. They were in their own world of weaponry—half impressed with the power they got from merely holding the rusted out rifles, and half trying to suppress the memories of the hundreds of soldiers that often crept back into their psyches as if on a repeating film reel.

Snapping out of his daydream, Lesio turned to Lyiubcyhk. "Let's go," he said. "Mama and Tato will be looking for us and they'll worry if we don't catch up."

Lyiubchyk obediently threw down his rifle but, as he often did, grabbed another soldier's medal that he found solidified in the clay of the riverbank. He quickly brushed it off in the shallow water he was standing beside and shoved it in his pocket.

He ran behind Lesio as the two darted under the arms and through the legs of the crowd as they made their way to the other side and began to scan the scene for the rest of their family.

A mere moment later, they heard shrieks and the cracking of the beams under the heavy weight of the festivalgoers. The bridge gave one final sigh before forsaking the task it had so stalwartly assumed all these years and crashing loudly in a heap on to the river below.

In its demise it took with it hundreds of innocent victims who had been trying to cross just a moment before, many of the very people Lyiubchyk and Lesio had dodged and sur-passed in an effort to catch up with their family. Had they lingered for even a moment longer, they surely would have been among those who had plunged to their deaths into the churning waters below.

In an hysterical panic, Petro, Iwan, and Daria with little Zvinusia sprinted in the direction of the screams and, fortu-nately for them all, were quickly staring at the boys as they were running away from what used to be the crowded bridge and into the arms of their parents.

●

So many times death had threatened to ensnare one, if not all, of their lives. It became more the norm for them to expect to cheat death than to live a life of constant worry. Life was hard, but for them to successfully get up each morning and greet another day they all had to hold each other tight when they could, suppress any memory of death's threat, and continue to hold any fatal menace at arm's length.

CHAPTER 22

The News

**The Zapar family sponsors, the Nenadkevych
family of Brooklyn, New York.**
Photo courtesy of the Zapar family.

*Our dream was finally coming true! At last we had sponsors from
America who were willing to assume responsibility for our family of
six, to help us get a fresh start and a new life in the New wwWorld.
The Nenadkevych family of Brooklyn, New York told us in a letter
that they saw the picture of our family in the newspaper with the*

petition seeking a sponsor. In response to this petition, they good-heartedly agreed to share their humble home with us and attend to our most immediate needs as immigrants.

A chain of events was set in motion for our departure from Germany: A trip to the American Consulate for final paperwork, necessary immunizations at a clinic, and packing up our few personal belongings and mementos from our burned home in Krywen'ke, as well as a few items we had acquired while living in Germany.

HAVING SUCCESSFULLY smuggled and saved the gold rubles that had been tucked beneath the wooden strip of the family's trunk, Iwan and Petro readied their belongings for the trip. Still not able to fully believe it was going to come to fruition, they basically went through the motions on the off chance that it would.

Iwan, Petro and Daria began to sell off what they couldn't take with them and to give away certain items to other families still waiting for news of passage, families that could definitely use them.

They were able to procure one suitcase apiece in which to pack their most valuable belongings and they all began to decide what they wanted or needed to take to this new land of opportunity.

Were the streets really paved with gold? Was this really a free society in which they would be able to pursue their own dreams? The thought of having any dream other than survival seemed too inconceivable for them to fully comprehend.

Supposedly, they would be experiencing this enchanted land in a few short weeks so the task of readying themselves to leave was now expedited to their top priority.

Daria was going through her things when she came across a kilim given to her at her wedding by her mother and father. In those days in Eastern Europe these kilims, intricately woven woolen tapestries that typically represented a pattern of one's home village, were given at weddings as part of the bride's *dowry* and often would be hung up in the couple's new house. Since Daria and Iwan were forced to flee not long after their wedding, they didn't have the luxury of hanging their kilim in a house of their own. Being so precious to Daria, she had hastily grabbed it that day right before they fled the burning of their village. Ever since then, she had used it daily in the back of that covered wagon to help keep them warm. Each time they moved she would fold the rectangular throw back up and cram it into their trunk. While, to both she and Iwan, it had continually grown to symbolize their union and those they left behind, it also grew in importance to them as they fled their homeland and now the entire continent on which they had been raised. It was a symbol of who they were and who they had become, but most importantly, it was one of the last symbols they had of their true identity as Ukrainians. It was not only a symbol but a link to their past—a past in which now, moving forward into their new life, was marred not only by the pain of their agonizing experiences, but by the unintentional scars and battle wounds caused by choices that had resulted in the necessary separation from their loved ones—their parents and grandparents who would never be forgotten. This kilim not only transcended its useful purpose, but had also garnered a life of its own as it made it through the same life events that Daria and Iwan did. When she was feeling that she needed her own parents near her, Daria would take her fingers and slowly rub them over the flourishes and emblems entwined in the threads. It was as if a piece of them existed there. And when she wrapped it around her own shoulders, or over the shoulders of her family, it was as if they were there with their arms around them all, protecting them in their love.

Daria brought the kilim up to her lips and softly kissed it. Then she held it to her breast for a second before one final sigh snapped her back to the task at hand. She wished her parents could see how strong she had become and how her family had returned time and time again from the grips of disaster and had arrived at the brink of this new life in America. America! Even the sound of it made Daria's heart flutter.

She turned to her children and, just like the kilim, wrapped herself around them and held them tight. "My dears. Freedom is almost in sight."

•

After weeks of packing and bittersweet time spent with their newly acquired German friends and confidants, they said their grateful goodbyes to Frau Zimmerman and her children and a very special goodbye to Frau Zimmerman's father. They all tried to hold back their nervous laughter when the old man proclaimed his need to *take a piss*.

CHAPTER 23

The Voyage

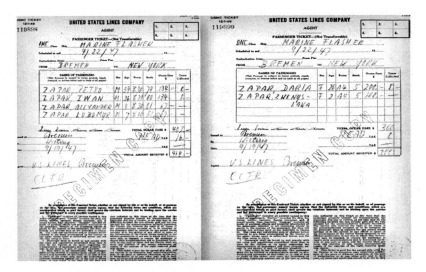

The Zapar family tickets for the SS Marine Flasher.
Photo courtesy of the Zapar family.

One more cross-country train trip was necessary—from Kempten to the port city of Bremen, where we would embark on our transatlantic voyage to America. The train wheels on the steel tracks could not click fast enough, as we felt like we were outrunning something which was about to grab us—and that all the good we were expecting to come to us would all just be a dream ending in great disappointment by the morning.

But the dream did not end—reality overtook us when we saw the ship we were about to board. The SS Marine Flasher was about to become our new home for the two-week voyage across the Atlantic. It was by no means a luxury cruise ship. It had been used for troop transport during the war and, although it was painted the traditional and dingy Navy gray, to us it was beautiful beyond words.

It seemed like we were boarding a floating city with several thousand immigrants like us. We found our bunks to be very cramped quarters but were delighted to finally be on board. Each family in our company aboard the ship had surely endured its own private hell and everyone undoubtedly felt the same longing for the promises this new land would offer.

The ship left port on September 22, 1947, in relatively calm seas, with its passengers all excited and looking forward to their journey towards a new life in America.

AS WITH THEIR journey thus far, life on the boat was not without incident. The seas did not remain calm for long and several days into the trip Daria awoke in the middle of the night screaming hysterically that Zvinusia had disappeared. Since she was only two-and-a-half years old at the time, she still slept very much under her mother's wing in their bunk each night. Daria would fall asleep with her tucked tightly under her arm every evening—they both drifted off to the rocking and swaying of the boat.

Upon awaking and not finding Zvinusia in bed with her, and irrationally ramping up her paranoia to fear that someone had kidnapped her, Daria began to scream in panic that her daughter had been stolen.

Iwan and Petro began to search with Daria until the entire quarters were wide awake and searching too. Several minutes ticked away with no sign of the toddler, until one fellow shipmate finally shouted, "I've found her!"

Daria rushed over to find her delicately sleeping daughter curled up in a ball, sound asleep and unaware of the commotion her disappearance had caused the entire area. As best as they could tell, the increasing strength of the waves the *Marine Flasher* was encountering on their voyage had caused Zvinusia to fall out of the bunk and make a continual roll across the floor until she had reached the opposite corner and come to a halt under another bed. Once calm was restored, the passengers returned to their bunks and continued to try to get whatever sleep they could in spite of the endless bouncing of the ship through the ocean's currents.

From then on, Daria slept facing the side of the ship at all times with Zvinusia tightly gripped in her arms, her little nose nearly pressed to the wall in front of her.

●

The next hurdle the Zapars had to overcome was the ensuing seasickness they all succumbed to in response to the continual and extreme roughness of the sea below the ship. Everyone, that was, except for Lesio, who was somehow able to delay his turn at sickness until his arrival in America, when he would be stricken with what could be called *lack of motion* sickness.

The stench of the resulting vomit caused most of the shipmates to opt to spend as much time above deck in the open ocean air as they possibly could. Already missing the rolling hills around their German village, Lyiubchyk and Lesio made do running the decks of the SS Marine Flasher, dodging in and out of deck chairs and petticoats, trying not to slip on the mist-stained steel surface.

During their transatlantic voyage they were fortunate not to encounter any major storms at sea and for the most part the ship stayed on course for New York. The only setback came a few days in when a rogue wave struck the ship's bow just at one of those times that the boys were darting through the main deck. As the ship swayed to the force of the wave, Lyiubchyk was knocked back and fell hard, hitting his temple on the steel deck and losing consciousness.

"Brother! Brother! Wake up!" Lesio cried as he shook his brother's shoulders. Not getting a response, he screamed, "Help! My brother is hurt. Someone please help us!"

A crowd rushed over to survey what had happened. Lyiubchyk's seemingly lifeless body resisted any attempts at revival. A few seconds later Iwan and Petro came upon the scene. Looks of terror flashed across both of their faces as they realized it was Lyiubchyck lying there before their eyes.

"Father!" Lesio screamed. "Help Lyiubchyk! I don't know what happened to him. One minute we were playing and running and the next he fell down and I can't wake him up."

With a demeanor of calm that eclipsed the panic he felt in his chest, Iwan began to smack at Lyiubchyk's cheeks in an attempt to revive the child. After a few moments of continual effort to revive Lyiubchyk, Iwan scooped up his limp body and set off towards the ship's infirmary. Petro and Lesio followed closely behind. Fortunately, Daria and Zvinusia had been napping in their bunk and were blissfully ignorant of the scene that was unfolding above.

Inside the infirmary, the Doctor was able to revive Lyiubchyk with smelling salts. As Lyiubchyk came to, he had a panic in his voice as he cast a stare directly through Iwan. "Father! I can't see!" He struggled to open his eyes wider and wider but darkness had enveloped his vision. "I can't see."

He was moving his eyes slowly and purposefully from left to right. Then he tried to stare up at the ceiling. He blinked hard and rubbed his eyes but nothing was helping.

The doctor began to shine his flashlight in Lyiubchyk's pupils and could see that they were not responding properly. With a look of sheer concern, he said, "Sir, only time will tell the extent of your son's damage. He needs as much rest as he can possibly get right now but I'm afraid there is nothing that I can do for him. There is a possibility that he could have hit his head so hard that his vision has been compromised. Take him back to his bunk and ensure that he do nothing but rest as peacefully as possible. Son," he said, turning to Lyiubchyk, "you are very lucky that you weren't hurt more than you were. That must have been one nasty spill you took. I don't think you will be blind, just wait for the darkness to lift. And the only thing that can help you now is time and rest. So promise me that you will follow that prescription, will you?"

"Yessir," responded Lyiubchyk, still wearing an astonished look on his face. By this time, Lesio had tears streaming down his cheeks. His arms were trembling as he grabbed his brother's hand.

"Come, brother. Let's go lie down." And, as always, their steps were quickly synchronized as Lesio guided Lyiubchyck back to his bunk.

Slowly but surely the darkness retreated. As the hours passed it was just as if someone was slowly opening the aperture on a camera and eventually the world went from dark forms and shapes to clarity. They were all elated that their latest crisis had resolved itself on its own.

Perhaps, in the universal order of things, this was the world's way of telling them that life was going to unfold in their favor. And, while things would still, at times, be out of their control or beyond the authority of their decision-making processes, time was on their side. And, perhaps, luck would continue to be, too.

CHAPTER 24

America

Towards evening on October 2, 1947, the SS Marine Flasher entered New York Harbor. Our three-year, seemingly nightmarish journey was finally over! We were thankful to God and the aide of our numerous angels along the way that our family was intact. We had survived!

AMERICA! JUST THE sound of it was enough to make all the Zapars smile. As the SS Marine Flasher drifted closer and closer to shore and to their new life, the family stood with their hands on the cold steel rails of the ship, staring into the breeze as this new land grew bigger and bigger in front of them. Several of *The Others* that had suffered similar war stories stood by their sides in a forced, yet secure feeling of unity and uncertainty.

Iwan and Petro stood shoulder to shoulder, each with a firm grasp on the rail. The breezes blew through their now thinning hair and the warm sun seemed to pierce through their clothing, awakening the butterflies in their stomachs. Petro, finding it hard to take his eyes off the sight of the harbor that lay ahead of them, finally turned just enough to catch his brother's expression out of the corner of his eye.

"Can you believe it, brother? Do you know how many times I have awoken from this very dream, only to find myself back in the cold grips of war and strife? But this feels different. I keep thinking I am going to wake up, but, for the first time in over a decade, I can honestly say that I already feel awake—completely awake and alive. But still, in the back of my head it feels irrational to think that this view before me is real. We shouldn't be here. We were never any better than all those people we watched die before our eyes." Then Petro asked the question they all had been quietly processing in their own way for the past few days. "Why us?"

"Petro," Iwan said with a shake of his head, "I have no clue *why us*. But this feeling I have is different, too. While I don't understand why or how we got so lucky, I feel like why *not* us? There were so many close calls and we all could have died—*should have died*, many times over. Life is unexplainable and only one day when our time really does come will we be able to fully understand. All I know is that sight stretched out before us is beautiful. It means freedom for us, but even more than that, it means safety. Before, we only had trees and forests between us, and *them,* but now we have the depth of the ocean and the promise of this free and independent society.

"I will never forget where we came from, but I will not look back. Not only do we deserve this—we fought for this, we lost our mother and father for all of this—and Darushiu, he said, turning to his wife, you lost your Father, too—and it is both our newfound right as well as our solemn promise to those we left behind to make the most of this new life, and to live each day from here forward with the same fervent determination and zeal for life in general that got us here in the first place." And with that, he reached into the breast pocket of his jacket and wrapped his fingers around his most treasured piece of home. *His safety pin.*

•

Daria's soft brown curls blew through the breeze under the scarf she had fashioned around her head to keep the cool breezes blowing off the autumn waters from chilling her to her now frail bones. That scarf was one of the few things they had left to remind them of how far they had come...it was made from the scraps of the wind-torn linen wagon covering that had once blocked out the winter snow as they plowed their way from village to village and through the forests of one country into the cobbled streets of another.

Daria rested one hand on that scarf to ensure that it wouldn't blow into the sea and the other on the shoulder of Zvinusia, as the two quietly stood with their hands on the steel railing. Zvinusia was peeking through the slats at this strange land that lay just ahead as it was coming into view. Daria couldn't help but think back to what that fortuneteller had said so many years ago: "...Know that there is nothing left. No reason for you to go back." While she knew she would always miss home, she was resolved to make this her new home now. And finally, she and her beloved family would be free of the dark clouds that had stalked them for so long.

From time to time Daria would still feel a twinge of heartache when she thought about Ukraine and her little village in Krywen'ke—and especially of her father she had to leave behind. But somehow, through their travels and all those hours she lay processing her life in the back of that wagon, she had settled her thoughts on making the most of this new life and this new path that was now laid out so crystal clear before her. She realized, as she stood at the bow of the ship that, while Ukraine would always hold a special place in her heart and soul, her life on the run had quickly outgrown what it could offer. Through all her years as a refugee and as her path had unfolded before her eyes, she had been overtaken by the determination to continue her forward march away from the oppressors she had worked so hard to escape. She must move into the metaphorical sun's rays that shone on this new promised land.

Still trying to believe that this was becoming a reality, Daria was finally able to understand the fortuneteller's prophecy. For the first time in years, she was excited about what lay before her. And while the demons would still haunt her from time to time and for the rest of her life, she was able to be happy and know that she could work to make her family happy, too. It wasn't going to be an easy road but it was going to be her road now. Hard choices would have to be made, yes, but at least there would be no more wagons carrying her and her children huddled up inside them, freezing cold and wrapped in torn blankets—and no more enemy soldiers choosing outcomes and making choices on her behalf and against her will.

•

Lyiubchyk and Lesio did what they always did. They stood side by side, too, just as their father and uncle always had, unified for the rest of their days in the strife and struggles that had molded them in those first tender years of their lives.

There were no more tears to shed and for the most part, their youthful optimism had vanquished the constant worry they had suffered during life in the wagon. One look in their eyes and it was apparent that their joy and overwhelming hope had spilled over to their expressions.

Lyiubchyk's eyes were closed, as if imagining what this new world would look like on the other side of the now shrinking expanse of water between it and their ship. Lesio's forward gaze seemed to be calculating how many new forts and buildings he could erect in this place called New York City. Even though they were still young, just seven and nine now, for the first time they, too, were able to feel that elusive sensation of pure, unspoiled happiness.

•

Here, as the family stood, shoulder-to-shoulder and side-by-side, in their golden hour of sunshine—yet alongside all the ghosts of all *The Others*—they all collectively *got it*. They felt *it* and *it* was hope. After feeling more defined by their struggles than by their possibilities for so long, they realized that this first step off the boat and onto this new soil of liberty was where their true life's story would begin. And now, they were ready. For them, the life they all had *earned* had *finally* begun.

The End

Epilogue

**The Zapar family living the American Dream on the
steps of their new home in Dorothy, NJ, 1951.**
Photo courtesy of the Zapar Family.

ONCE IN AMERICA, this remarkable family took advantage
of every opportunity that came across their path, being forever
grateful to be in this enchanting new land. They felt compelled to help others like themselves, who still were at risk of
repatriation to the Soviets and needed sponsorship in order to

immigrate to the United States. During this time of need by other displaced persons, they would help sponsor over forty families across the Atlantic.

While living in New York City, they took full advantage of the life and culture it offered, however, having an innate entrepreneurial spirit, they decided around 1950 that they would turn their ambitions to starting their own business. With little more than his word and a handshake, Iwan procured financial assistance from several of his friends and was able to purchase a ten-acre parcel of land in Dorothy, New Jersey. There they would launch a poultry business and build a simple yet sturdy home.

Just like most immigrants at the time, the family was struggling financially. It took all six family members to run the chicken farm, working countless hours grading the eggs, grinding chicken feed and all the various farming chores that came along with the business. Iwan even took a second job constructing new homes for other European transplants in an effort to bring in more money for the family.

After realizing poultry farming wasn't giving them the stability they needed, and growing tired of the never ending hours of work, that entrepreneurial flame was lit once again. In short order they built Zapar's Service Station of Dorothy on the front of their land, which, as luck would have it faced an increasingly busy road. They ran the station and a small general store with Daria helping to run a luncheonette that was later incorporated into the business. They did their best and continued to work long, hard hours and, in the mid-70's, after a few other odd jobs and many ups and downs, Daria and Iwan would finally find time to slow down and enjoy some well-deserved rest. But their time to bask in this slower pace of life did not last long.

Daria awoke on the morning of April 11, 1977, to find that Iwan had died in his sleep. Since that day, she has been convinced that he was having another one of his war-induced nightmares, perhaps running in fear yet again from the evil Communist henchmen, ultimately causing his heart to beat uncontrollably until it simply gave out.

Nevertheless, Daria's strong will and passion for life has continued on and, at present day, she just celebrated her 93rd birthday. She enjoys time with her children, grandchildren and great grandchildren and lives life to the fullest. To this day, she is petrified of snow. The experience at the Hungarian border left a fear in her core that she simply cannot escape.

Lesio, Lyiubchyk and Zvinusia have all had their turn at the American dream. Lesio began his service to this new country in the United States Air Force and has remained a master builder of 'things,' consulting in the field of energy conservation and sustainability and currently living "off-the-grid" in the Alleghany Mountains of New York. Both Lyiubchyk and Zvinusia would earn college degrees and spend countless years giving back to their communities through education—Lyiubchyk, as an administrator in the public school system and Zvinusia as a teacher for children with disabilities. All would raise their own families and enjoy both the stability the United States had to offer and the endless opportunities it afforded their children. It was clear that even though they all should have died many times during their life on the run, the universe had a greater plan for each of them.

On December 17, 2012, Lyiubchyk drew a final breath, as he could not out run his battle with an aggressive form of lymphoma. Today, his words and his documentation of his family's struggles will remain one of his greatest gifts.

And then there's Petro. Throughout this book, and their lives together, Petro was always the 'supporting actor' in the near shadows, or, when circumstances of desperation needed him to step up, he rose to the forefront. He was a valued confidant, a source of strength, and, once in America he exerted countless hours of physical labor with Iwan and Daria, in helping them build their new life in Dorothy.

After helping Iwan and Daria establish the poultry farm, he moved to Florida where he met and married his wife, Justine. They would eventually move to San Diego, California, where he worked at Ryan Aircraft Company until his retirement. On April 9, 1992, at the age of 84, he passed away in San Diego.

In the early 1970's Iwan and Petro were able to locate their mother, while also finding out that their father had indeed perished in a Siberian labor camp. Their mother had been held captive for years in those same camps. Upon her release she was not allowed to return to her village for fear of it creating 'sympathizers.' Tired of the cold and physically worn out she decided to move to Crimea for the warmer climate. Her sons filled out the paperwork to bring her to America, but days before she was to get on an airplane headed to the U.S., she was found dead. Both Iwan and Petro always believed there was more to her death. They hypothesized that she was told she needed immunizations to enter the new country and, instead, was euthanized from one of the inoculations so that word of her forced slavery to the Communists wouldn't reach the free states. This evoked even more fear in the brothers and further instilled in them that their '*crime*' would never be forgotten. They never returned to Ukraine.

The bond between the two brothers was so tight and their love so great that they truly personified the saying, "when one is hurting, the other is crying." Today, both brothers are buried beside each other in a Ukrainian Cemetery in South Bound Brook, New Jersey—two brothers under one gravestone.

Etched on that stone are the words, "*In hopeful dreams of freedom for Ukraine.*"

Acknowledgements

I AM DEEPLY GRATEFUL to every person that has believed in my writing, believed in this book and has been there through this journey called life. Scott Cohen, Eliza Cohen, Quinn Cohen, Greg Zapar, Stacy Zapar, Maddie Zapar, Collin Zapar, Linda Jo Zapar, Lisande Champeau, Cameron Champeau, Howard Cohen, Martha Reagan, Rebecca Reagan and the McCullough family—thank you for being here through it all and most importantly for being family. As the family circle becomes smaller and smaller it's something I'm even more grateful for every day.

To my brother Greg, this whole thing called life has been such a journey of love and loss and as a big brother, they don't get any better than you. I won the sibling jackpot.

Doug Ellis, Jr, Jason Borte, Derrick Borte, and Sharon Cooper, thank you for taking the concept of this novel seriously even when there were few pages written, and for your suggestions and gracious advice that helped to improve every aspect of this book. And a special thank you to Randy Kaplan for taking on this editing project and for your true craftsmanship of the writing process.

Thank you to Daria Zapar Baron, Zweneslava Zapar Clem and Alex Zapar for graciously letting me share the family story one chapter at a time.

Thank you to those who will never be able to read this book but have shaped it into what it has become through your lessons on love and life: Cornelia Straub Zapar, Dorothy Lackey Straub, William Herman Straub, Janet Cohen, Charles Harold Reagan. I miss each of you every day but never forget the love and life lessons you infused in my upbringing.

Iwan Zapar and Petro Zapar, thank you for being the foundation for who we are today. And thank you for silently showing all of us that the right path isn't always the easiest but hope is even larger than despair.

And finally, Lubomyr Zapar, while your voice is missing your words still live on. Thank you for fighting until the very end. Thank you for showing us the value of every breath and giving us the stubborn will to succeed down the path of our own choosing.

GINNY ZAPAR COHEN is a blogger, an entrepreneur, a freelance graphic designer, a mom and a chronic overachiever fueled by life, family losses and her coffee addiction. She is an activist for children with disabilities as co-director of Surfers Healing Virginia Beach, taking kids with autism surfing, and a runner for Team Hoyt VB, which pushes children with disabilities in road races. Through her blogging and writing she strives to capture the inspiring slices of the human spirit with her raw and heart felt prose. Her accomplishments include a brief stint as the third grade spelling bee champion, her recognition as one of the "Ten Most Beautiful Women of Hampton Roads" in 2011 for her contributions to the community, and paddle boarding 26 miles around the island of Manhattan.

For more insight into the book, read Ginny Zapar Cohen's blog at **www.GinnyZaparCohen.com**

Follow on Facebook: **GZCohen1**
Follow on Twitter: **@ginnyzaparcohen**
Follow on Instagram: **@ginnycohen**

Lubomyr "Lou" Zapar

LOU WAS A BORN leader and the first in his family to go to college. He proudly graduated from Virginia Polytechnic Institute & State University with a degree in Business Administration and enjoyed his time on campus as a Squadron Commander for the Corps of Cadets. He found no use for computers or social media but rather, kept his hands busy creating beautiful pieces of furniture. He was an assistant principal by day—shaping the lives of middle school children for decades—and a master craftsman by night, turning out beautiful antique reproductions for Colonial Williamsburg through his company, Heirloom Furniture. Prior to his death, he completed his handwritten account of the Zapar family's story, the account on which Talabarske is based, titled, "*Our Bonus Lives.*"

CPSIA information can be obtained at www.ICGtesting.com
Printed in the USA
BVOW08s1042271113

337503BV00002B/60/P